Tik-Tun

Jaunt

Striiker

Lochlan

For Mom and Dad

SHARK WARS

EJ ALTBACKER

INTO THE Abyss

razOr
bill

An Imprint of Penguin Group (USA) Inc.

Shark Wars #3: Into the Abyss

RAZORBILL

Published by the Penguin Group
Penguin Young Readers Group
345 Hudson Street, New York, New York 10014, U.S.A.
Penguin Group (USA) Inc., 375 Hudson Street, New York, New York 10014, U.S.A.
Penguin Group (Canada), 90 Eglinton Avenue East, Suite 700, Toronto, Ontario, Canada M4P 2Y3
(a division of Pearson Penguin Canada Inc.)
Penguin Books Ltd, 80 Strand, London WC2R 0RL, England
Penguin Ireland, 25 St Stephen's Green, Dublin 2, Ireland
(a division of Penguin Books Ltd)
Penguin Group (Australia), 250 Camberwell Road, Camberwell, Victoria 3124, Australia
(a division of Pearson Australia Group Pty Ltd)
Penguin Books India Pvt Ltd, 11 Community Centre, Panchsheel Park, New Delhi – 110 017, India
Penguin Group (NZ), 67 Apollo Drive, Mairangi Bay, Auckland 1311, New Zealand
(a division of Pearson New Zealand Ltd)
Penguin Books (South Africa) (Pty) Ltd, 24 Sturdee Avenue, Rosebank,
Johannesburg 2196, South Africa

Penguin Books Ltd, Registered Offices: 80 Strand, London WC2R 0RL, England

10 9 8 7 6 5 4 3 2 1

Copyright © 2012 Razorbill

ISBN 978-1-59514-382-2

Library of Congress Cataloging-in-Publication Data is available

Printed in the United States of America

INTO THE **Abyss**

CHAPTER 1

GRAY TORE THROUGH THE WATER, MINDLESS OF the shrieking crowd all around him. His concentration was total as his huge opponent barreled forward using an attacking move called Spearfisher Streaks by the Cliffs. Gray feinted left before slipping into Swordfish Parries. There was a tremendous shock down Gray's spine as his snout struck the flank of the ferocious great white. A solid hit!

The crowd's yells and excited thrashing vibrated the water so intensely that his hearing and lateral line senses were nearly useless. But the battlefield was well-lit and that wasn't the problem. No, the problem lay in the fact that there was absolutely no quit in his foe, who recovered quickly and zoomed straight at him once again.

I didn't even slow him down, thought Gray, gnashing his rows of curved, razor-sharp teeth in frustration.

The great white was wickedly agile, carving turns

through the water that Gray was hard-pressed to deflect or defend. But he had learned much in the months since the Battle of Riptide.

"Come on, come on," Gray muttered to himself. "I know you want to do it." The huge shark tried Yellowfin Feeding on Minnows, which Gray ruined by using Waving Greenie. Then the great white went for a Topside Rip, which was a deadly dorsal fin attack. But Gray knew this was a trick. And sure enough, at the last moment the charging shark switched into his favorite move—the one Gray had been waiting for him to attempt—Orca Bears Down.

Gotcha! Gray thought triumphantly. He rolled into a rising current, madly churning his tail to shift sideways just enough that the hurtling shark missed him by a fin length. Then Gray streaked after the great white and performed the very same move.

There was a satisfying "Oof!" from Gray's opponent as he was driven into the seabed. With a tail waggle, he signaled surrender. The match was over.

Gray had finally won. He had finally beaten King Lochlan boola Naka Fiji, and it was glorious!

"Yes! Yes! I knew you were coming with Orca Bears Down!" Gray exclaimed triumphantly as Lochlan spat sand from his mouth.

"Went to that feeding ground once too often, eh? Oh, I'm going to be tasting the seabed for a week! Good match, though!" Loch replied with an embarrassed grin.

Gray flexed his pectoral fins. "I don't blame you for trying. You've beaten me, like, twenty times with it!"

The crowd chanted, "Gray! Gray! Gray!" He waved his tail to everyone in the stadium, acknowledging the cheers. His mother Sandy the nurse shark was there, as were his younger brother and sister, Riprap and Ebbie. Gray felt his heart nearly burst when he saw how proudly they looked at him. He had been shocked when he learned he wasn't technically related to them—he was a megalodon, a different sort of prehistore shark-kind that supposedly died off millions of years ago. But Sandy was the only mother Gray had ever known and that was what mattered. In the same way, he was Rip-rap and Ebbie's (oddly large) big brother. For now Gray told them—and everyone else—that he was a rare type of reef shark. Only his closest friends knew his megalodon secret.

They too were watching the action, so he swam over to them. Striiker was fighting next, Gray saw. If there was fighting to be done, Striiker—Gray's first in Line—would be there. But the rest of his Five in the Line—Shell, Mari, Snork, and Barkley—preferred to hover and watch. These five were his best and closest friends in the Big Blue and had swum flank to flank with him since the very beginning, when Gray had been banished from Coral Shiver. The adventures they had been through! From being forced to join the shiver of the ferocious great white Goblin, to stopping his plan to take over the North Atlantis at the Tuna Run, and then banding together with King Lochlan and the formidable fins of AuzyAuzy Shiver to drive the wicked emperor Finnivus and his Black Wave armada from their territory—it was amazing that they were still around to enjoy this fine day.

But the thought of Finnivus made Gray remember there were important things to do today. "I have to go with Lochlan," Gray told Barkley, Sandy, and the others when he saw the golden great white gesture with his tail for him to follow. "I'll meet you all later!"

Gray swam away from the crowd to join Lochlan. He felt a small electric charge roll through the water as Prime Minister Shocks motioned Striiker and an Auzy-Auzy mariner forward for their match with a flick of the tail from his flexible eel body. This electricity was especially useful when Shocks wanted everyone's attention, like at dweller council meetings, where things could get a little shouty. And when all else failed, the Prime Minister's full charge packed quite a wallop. After a few instructions to tell both combatants to keep it clean and bloodless, Shocks let off another bolt of electricity to signal the start of the match. Gray and Lochlan swam off, the shouts of the excited crowd rolling with them as they glided from the training field to their meeting with the leaders of Hammer and Vortex Shivers.

Gray sighed, finally able to relax a little. He was glad the match was over. He liked training, of course. But this felt more like fighting to entertain others. Something was just not right about that. Not when so much blood had been spilled in the last year. But taking back the Riptide homewaters from Finnivus and his armada demanded some celebration, even if it was a few months later. And Lochlan had told Gray that he needed to prove his worth in front of the two other shivers that were here to consider joining their cause.

It was true that Finnivus and the Indi armada had been chased away to their homewaters. But the hateful emperor would be back to seek vengeance. It wasn't a matter of *if*, but *when*. That was why Lochlan had sent messengers to Hammer and Vortex Shivers. "Besides," Lochlan told Gray, "we really should break in the place with a bang-o, doncha think?"

To Gray's thinking, this whole week had been one heck of a bang-o. After a long and often boisterous council meeting, Gray had decided to resurrect Riptide Shiver, combining his old shiver, Coral, with the Line from Rogue Shiver, as well as with any friendly shark-kind displaced by Finnivus and his warring. Riptide had been an ancient and honorable shiver for thousands of years before Goblin, its previous leader, came along and named it after *himself*. "In a few years, no one will even remember that flipper," Striiker had insisted at the council meeting, and everyone had voted for their combined shivers to bring the name of Riptide Shiver back into being.

Coral still existed, technically, with Quickeyes the thresher as their leader, Onyx the blacktip as his first, and Gray's mom Sandy as his second, but they decided they weren't the fins to lead the battle against Finnivus and graciously gave up their own positions to join Riptide as shiver sharks. Riptide United was the name of the force that would swim out to battle Finnivus, though it was not yet determined how many shivers would participate.

Long-range scouts had confirmed to Gray, Lochlan, and their military advisor Whalem that Finnivus was still in the far-off Indi Shiver homewaters. They could breathe easy, at least for a little while, and so they were having this party. Lochlan had told Gray it was a *working* party. They would try to gain allies during the festivities. Most everyone else treated it like a party-party, though.

I wish I could, thought Gray.

Underneath the laughter and excitement of the celebration, Gray felt a dreadful tingle in the water. It was a sensation of danger lurking, not close right now, but coming for sure.

It had been six months since the combined forces of AuzyAuzy, Coral, and Rogue Shivers had defeated the Indi armada and sent Emperor Finnivus frantically swimming all the way to the Indi Ocean and his own homewaters. Finnivus was a cruel and vicious tiger shark, the leader of an ancient shiver that wanted to conquer all the Big Blue. The emperor had been miraculously bested, but Finnivus wasn't the type of fish to forgive and forget. He would return to wipe them out. And that was why, even though today's celebration was fun, Gray couldn't shake the feeling in the water that seemed to whisper: *Watch your tails, everyone. Watch your tails.*

Gray glanced at Lochlan, who told him, "Just hover and look tough. Remember, you can never say anything dumb if you keep your mouth shut."

"I'll let you do the talking," Gray said, giving the golden great white a bump. "But thanks for all the confidence." They swam toward the center of the homewaters and to Speakers Rock, the most impressive part of Riptide's ancient territory.

As word of the Battle of Riptide spread, sharkkind from all over the Big Blue had come to ask questions and seek alliances. Most were small shivers, much like the one Gray grew up in. They were untrained and would be wiped out in a fight against a true battle shiver like the Indi armada.

So Lochlan had invited the leaders of Hammer and Vortex, two powerful shivers, as his personal guests for the day, in an effort to convince them to directly join forces. Hammer and Vortex each had more than two hundred battle-hardened mariners. Riptide United desperately needed their numbers. Lochlan had experience with one of the two, Hammer Shiver; it was composed entirely of fearsome hammerheads with a leader named Grinder. They came from the North Sific.

The other shiver came from the faraway southern reaches of the Sific. Vortex's leader was a port jackson shark—a type Gray had never seen before—named Silversun. The odd fish had a blocky head and was brown on his upper half and white on the lower, with darker brown stripes highlighting the peculiar curves of his body.

Lochlan had told Gray that Silversun being a leader was interesting because port jackson sharks weren't very good in a fight. Now that he was approaching the shark himself, Gray could see why. Silversun was smaller than Barkley! He didn't even have *teeth*! Port jackson sharks apparently had a crushing plate to eat shellheads and even mollusks. Gray wondered how anyone would follow him into battle, and Lochlan, reading his mind, whispered, "There's obviously more than meets the eye with Silversun, so don't underestimate him." It was good advice. Besides, the rest of Silversun's Line was composed of very big sharkkind, indeed.

"I thought you never lost, Lochlan," drawled Grinder, the hammerhead leader.

The golden great white grinned, his rows of triangle teeth showing. "Sometimes it happens. I don't mind losing to friends, Grinder." Apparently, Hammer Shiver and AuzyAuzy had at one time warred against each other. But that was many, many years ago.

"Which is why you'd like to form an alliance," Silversun said, joining the conversation. "You're afraid you'll lose to Finnivus."

Gray wanted to immediately tell the weird little shark he better watch it—that Lochlan was afraid of *nothing*—but the great white flicked a fin for him to stay quiet. Loch then *nodded* to Silversun.

"Only a fool wouldn't fear a crazy fish taking control of the Big Blue. You managed to avoid a snout-to-snout scrumble with his armada so far. But if that evil tiger tightens his grip on your territories, it'll be the beginning of the end. For both of you. We'd be gone before that, of course. By ourselves we don't have a chance. But if we swim as one, we can form an immovable reef that Finnivus will crack his teeth on."

Gray marveled at Lochlan's commanding presence and powerful words. He would never have come up with such a great answer! But even with this reply, Gray saw that the two shiver leaders weren't ready to do a group rub just yet.

"Something to think about, I guess," Grinder replied. "Now, where can I get a bite to eat around here?"

Lochlan looked to Gray for the answer. "Umm, this time of day? Off the western side of the homewaters is best." The hammerhead grunted and left.

"Thank you for your hospitality." Silversun dipped his blocky head in a sign of respect for Lochlan. "I'll talk this over with my Line."

11

Lochlan watched the pair swim off. "That could have gone better," he said, shaking his own massive head from side to side.

"Better? If they don't see how they'd be a couple of complete chowderheads if they don't join us, I say we don't need them!"

Lochlan laughed. "Silversun is no chowderhead, and neither is Grinder. Like good leaders they want to keep their options open." Gray followed the golden great white as they swam back toward the main area of the celebration. "They want to do the best for their mariners, their families—"

Someone screamed!

Gray could smell blood in the water. His nerves jangled a warning up and down his spine. "Are we being attacked?" Gray asked Lochlan, a cold worry gripping the pit of his stomach. Was his mother okay? Were his friends? It was impossible to tell. Panicked sharkkind and dwellers were tearing through the water in all directions.

"This way," Lochlan ordered. "Cover my topside!"

Gray did a smart half roll and got into perfect position to guard the great white's dorsal fin. It took less than fifty strong tail strokes to get to the source of the blood.

It was a tiger shark from AuzyAuzy. Gray recognized him but didn't know his name. He was terribly wounded with a deep, ragged bite on his right flank.

"My King," he sputtered, looking at Lochlan, blood flowing between his notched teeth. "The Black Wave is coming. The Black Wave is coming . . . for you all."

Then the AuzyAuzy mariner's eyes rolled to the whites and he was gone.

CHAPTER 2

"DOUBLE OUR PATROLS!" SHOUTED LOCHLAN, taking control of the situation. "And find out what happened to the rest of Karten's team!"

Gray looked at the mauled tiger shark. So his name was Karten, he thought. Even though there were hundreds of AuzyAuzy mariners, Gray was ashamed for not having known.

"I'm afraid the rest of the patrol fared no better than this worthy," said Whalem, joining them. "Finnivus has been setting traps for our scouts." He grimaced in pain. In the months since the Battle of Riptide, it seemed that age was catching up with the former mariner prime of Indi Shiver. Gray and Lochlan tried to talk the battle-scarred tiger into less strenuous duties, but Whalem insisted on managing the patrol schedule as well as the long-range scouting missions.

"Finnivus wants to keep us blind and in the dark, like a cavefish," Lochlan said.

"The patrols will continue, My King," Whalem said. He bobbed his snout. This move caused another spasm of pain along with an audible crack of cartilage. "Excuse my complaining spine. I'll see to it at once!" Whalem swam off, but not very smoothly.

Lochlan shook his head. "That old finner is in a tidal wave of pain but still does more than half my best mariners. Gray, let's jaw about finding him an assistant later. Now, we should see about Grinder and Silversun. We don't want them taking this attack the wrong way."

"Which way is that?" asked Gray.

Lochlan frowned, flicking his tail. "That we're weak and our cause is hopeless."

Gray met later with Barkley and the rest of Rogue's Line: Striiker the great white, Mari the thresher, Shell the bull shark, and of course Snork the sawfish. The Five in a Line concept was created by Tyro, the First Fish, because the Big Blue could be a dangerous place. In times such as these, Gray was glad to know that in case he couldn't lead, someone else would be there to swim into his place. The group gathered after a hasty meeting with Hammer and Vortex Shivers. Lochlan assured both Grinder and Silversun that patrols would be tripled close to the Riptide homewaters and long-distance scouts would be sent out to make sure the Indi armada wasn't nearby.

The ancient and grand Speakers Rock meeting area of the Riptide homewaters was eerily empty. The small dwellers were keeping hidden and large ones such as whales and giant mantas hadn't visited since the Battle of Riptide.

Gray was still shaken by the grim message sent in the form of the mauled long-range scout. The Indi armada was readying itself to move, he just knew it. The only reason to take out their scouts—other than being vindictive—was to keep your own movements secret. Finnivus and his Black Wave were coming, and the waters would turn red with blood when they arrived.

Gray was so big that he could take care of himself against anyone or anything in the Big Blue. In fact, Barkley would tell me I could stand to lose a few pounds, Gray thought. No, he was scared for the others. How could he protect *everyone* he loved? His mother and the sharks he'd grown up with, his five best friends here, his new friends from AuzyAuzy—now all battle brothers and sisters—and a host of dwellers like Yappy and Prime Minister Shocks were at risk.

At least Gray was sure that Lochlan and his Line needed no protecting. And probably Takiza, who had suddenly left again without telling anyone. Where was the mysterious, magical betta? *He* could definitely take care of himself. But still. Gray didn't like the fact that everyone he knew was in danger. "How did it come to this?" he whispered.

"It's not your fault, Gray," Barkley answered. "It isn't anything we did. We're just alive and in the way."

Striiker bristled and slashed his crescent-shaped tail through the water in frustration. "Barkley's right. We didn't ask that big flipper Finnivus to swim halfway 'round the world and attack us!"

But Shell got to the truth of the matter. "We do seem to be smack in the middle of it, though."

Mari gave Gray a sympathetic rub on the flank with her long thresher tail. "With everything that's been heaped on you, it's okay to cry if you want."

"But *please* don't," Shell muttered, a little louder than he intended. Everyone laughed.

"What's so funny?" asked Snork. "I cry when I'm sad. It always makes me feel better."

"Of course you would, but Gray *can't!*" Striiker emphasized. "You're not a leader. Leaders don't get respect from other sharkkind by bawling their way around the Big Blue."

"Striiker, quit being a tailbender," Mari told the great white.

Snork didn't take offense. He waggled his serrated bill in agreement. "That's okay. I know I'm not tough. But I'm trying to learn!" The sawfish said this with such enthusiasm that it caused another round of laughter.

"So what's the latest with Hammer and Vortex

Shivers?" asked Barkley, because they hadn't been allowed in that meeting. The dogfish was smart. Probably the smartest fin Gray knew. It made hiding any setback extremely difficult.

Gray gave a noncommittal swish of his tail. "Those negotiations are moving forward with vigor, and Lochlan and I are expecting good news any day now."

Striiker looked at him quizzically along with everyone else. "What? Forward with *vigor*?"

Barkley sighed. "That was what Lochlan told Gray to say in case we asked."

"Sounds pretty good!" Snork remarked.

"Too bad it's a load of chum," Shell said in his dry way.

Mari swam forward. "Really? Lochlan wants you to lie to us? Your friends?"

"No, not lie. Not exactly," Gray hedged. "He just doesn't want anyone to know he's having a tough time getting them to join up . . . fully."

"Or at all," Barkley prodded.

"Or at all," Gray agreed before he could stop himself. "I mean—no, not that. Something else. Something better."

"We'll be crushed without their mariners if Finnivus comes with his full armada," Shell remarked. "We won't take them by surprise twice."

"Yeah, that's for sure," Striiker agreed. "The amount of training they must do. They are the nearest thing to perfect mariners in the Big Blue."

Mari bristled. "You *admire* them?"

"No. I *respect* them," Striiker said, without the usual sarcasm or scorn he mustered when speaking about Finnivus and Indi Shiver. "We all should."

Gray moved forward, halfway over Speakers Rock. "Maybe Grinder and Silversun would join up with Lochlan if they knew I was a megalodon?" Gray had learned the truth about his species from Velenka, the crafty mako who was now allied with Finnivus. Megalodons were thought to have died out millions of years ago. How Gray came to be here no one knew. Not even his mother, Sandy. She had rescued him when he was only a pup in a faraway ocean on a day when the very water was on fire, and mountains of rock were swallowed up by the Dark Blue in a gigantic seaquake.

For a moment there was only silence. Gray hoped everyone was speechless because his idea was so good.

"That's gotta be the dumbest, most idiotic thing I've ever heard," Barkley said, a tinge of awed amazement in his voice.

Striiker shook his massive head. "Nope, nope, you're giving the idea too much credit. It's the dumbest idea that *anyone* in the *entire* Big Blue has come up with."

"Don't forget about the past," Shell added. "It might also be the worst idea of all time."

"All right already!" Gray shouted. He was a little miffed. "I get it!" There had to be someone who was on his side. "Snork, what do you think?"

"It's an . . . interesting way to go," Snork began, before petering out.

"Wow, worst idea ever," Gray told everyone. "You must be so proud to have me as your leader."

Mari allowed herself to drift a bit closer with the current. "We wouldn't have it any other way."

Striiker surprised Gray by adding a strong, "You got that right. But telling others that you're a megalodon would cause—well, we don't know what it would cause, actually. But nothing good."

"I can guess," Barkley said. "It would cause confusion and nervousness, even outright panic. And we need exactly none of those right now. Lochlan would probably tell you the same thing. Don't worry, he'll convince Grinder and Silversun to join us."

Barkley's words made everyone feel a little bit better. Gray hoped his friend was right. He really did. Everything counted on Lochlan's persuasiveness and leadership. He had to succeed! Because Finnivus was coming, and the evil fish would stop at nothing to get his revenge on everyone Gray loved.

CHAPTER 3

VELENKA WATCHED AS THE INDI ARMADA SWEPT in and destroyed a pitiful force of prisoners—a captured shiver, a few Riptide scouts, and several sharkkind that had somehow displeased Finnivus in the past few weeks. One poor tiger shark was a mariner from the Indi armada. His mistake had been to *cough* during one of the emperor's speeches.

Though blood clouded the water, the three battle fins of the Indi armada worked together smoothly, never a tail stroke out of place. They executed the orders of the mariner prime flawlessly and without hesitation. There were only a few of the opposing force still alive, all clumped into a terrified ball. Any who tried to flee were ripped apart by the Indi mariners.

"Kill them all!" screamed Finnivus. "Every single one!"

The mariner prime, a middle-aged tiger shark, dipped

his head and obeyed. Ever since Gray had destroyed Indi Shiver's lantern fish signaler, the orders had to be relayed by fin signs, which weren't nearly as fast as the signaler. The previous mariner prime had also been killed by Gray at the battle whose name could not be spoken. That had not been a good day for Indi Shiver.

Moments after the command was shouted by Finnivus, it was over. Not a single one of the opposing hundred and fifty prisoners remained.

"Excellent!" yelled Finnivus. "Well done!"

The mariner prime took his place at the head of the Indi armada. Every shark in the armada held attention hover and then bobbed their heads to the emperor. The precision of so many performing the move exactly at the same time made an odd *fwumph* noise in the reddish water.

Finnivus allowed the warm current to gently push him into his throne built on top of the Speakers Rock directly in the center of the Indi homewaters. Velenka took in the sight as the emperor ordered various court sharks this way and that. Finnivus was a boastful young fin, but he hadn't been pulling her tail when he said the Indi homewaters were the most beautiful place in all the Big Blue. The royal court was arranged before him—at a lower depth, of course—and it had taken her breath away the first time she saw it. Crabs and urchins created glorious, colorful patterns that changed many times each day. Sometimes the designs were intricate lines done in the Indi colors. Other times they were spot-on representations of Finnivus himself, swimming or hunting! It was amazing.

Behind his throne were the fantastic Floating Greenie Gardens of Indi. Beautiful kelp, seaweeds, and undersea flowers bloomed constantly for the enjoyment of Finnivus and his father before him, and his father before that, all the way back to times unremembered. Walls of delicate coral had been built by master dwellers that could either stop the current or allow it to whisk the blooms upward and form a spectacular path. This was so that whenever Finnivus decided to have a swim, he would not see anything that *wasn't* beautiful.

It was truly the most wondrous place in the Big Blue, and Velenka wanted nothing more than to recline on the royal throne—which was made of lustrous, glowing corals that were regularly *polished* by sea snails! But the throne wasn't hers to rest on. It belonged to Finnivus Victor Triumphant, emperor of—almost—the entire Big Blue. Velenka could understand his passion to be ruler of all the waters. She loved power, too, more than anything. But why risk your life for one little area of the Atlantis if you controlled everything else?

Finnivus, though, was crazed with anger. He had been routed and his royal court forced to flee from the Riptide homewaters. The arrogant tiger shark couldn't just lean on his shining coral throne and relax. He would kill everyone who did not bow before him. And though the tiger emperor hated leaving the Indi homewaters, you couldn't conquer the seven seas if you stayed put, could you?

"This tastes terrible!" Finnivus yelled about his meal. "Bring me a fresh one this instant."

"Immediately, Your Magnificence!" answered Tydal, the first court fish, as he whisked off to get another seasoned bass. The brown and yellow epaulette shark was in charge of the details in the court. Tydal was undoubtedly very good at his job to have survived this long.

Velenka knew that there was nothing wrong with the sea bass. The dwellers responsible for seasoning it would never have sent it from the preparation area if there was even the slightest doubt about its deliciousness. This was just Finnivus working himself into another mood about his favorite topic of hatred—Gray.

"They were only prisoners," Finnivus muttered to himself about the recently concluded battle exercise.

Velenka didn't react. Neither did anyone else in court. It was better to be sure you *had* to answer than to casually put forward an opinion. That could get you eaten. Or placed with the prisoners for the armada to practice on. Finnivus cast a glance directly at her from his throne. "Velenka. They were prisoners," he said.

There was no avoiding this any longer. "Your Majesty?" she asked, dipping her head respectfully.

Finnivus sighed as if she were a pup, too stupid to understand. "The sharks my armada just demolished—they were *only* prisoners."

"That were caught by your invincible armada," Velenka said. "They had no choice in the matter." It wasn't the response he wanted, but it was enough of an answer to keep her out of trouble.

"Yes, of course," groused Finnivus. "But what I mean is that mere prisoners are hardly an acceptable substitute for the mariners which Gray and Lochlan will have when I—umm, *we*, obliterate them."

Well, of course they aren't! Velenka thought to herself. These prisoners were hungry and tired. Beaten. No match for the finely tuned Indi armada. It would have been disastrous to suggest that, though, which was why she chose to play dumb.

"Any practice will make your mighty mariners even better," Velenka soothed. "And there is no fighting force in the Big Blue that can match the Indi armada. You will one day go to Riptide and conquer what is rightfully yours!"

But not if I can convince you otherwise, she thought.

There was a smattering of agreement from the other sharkkind in the court, but only after Finnivus nodded and clicked his notched teeth together. "You are very smart for a fin from the boonie-greenie," Finnivus said, turning to the court, who all laughed as if this were the funniest thing they had ever heard. Velenka bobbed her head once more and smiled, flashing her own pointy, white teeth. How she hated playing the sea toady to anyone. Even to Finnivus Victor Triumphant, Emperor of the Big Blue.

"You are right! My armada has no equal!" exclaimed Finnivus. "And soon, I will exact my revenge on everyone in the North Atlantis, but Lochlan and Gray most of all!" Everyone cheered. "*If* they are still alive when my armada faces theirs—" Finnivus smiled as if at some secret thought. Velenka wondered what he might be hiding. "They will be captured! Then, oh then, they will watch as we exact our justice for their treachery by sending every single fin they care for to the Sparkle Blue before their very eyes!"

"Wonderful! Wonderful!" Velenka exclaimed along with the sharks that crowded closer to Speakers Rock.

While it was tricky to swim the currents in the court, Velenka knew Finnivus liked her. This was important as it saved her from being eaten unless she did something very stupid. And her mother didn't raise a dumb shellhead for a daughter. Court life was a plush and lazy lifestyle, filled with the best of everything! Why take the chance of ruining it by going to war? But Finnivus thought of nothing else. As soon as he was safely in the Indi homewaters, he set to calling mariners from all around the seven seas to join his *Armada of Justice*, as he called it. The Black Wave now numbered in the thousands. There was no way that any in the Atlantis would survive the emperor's royal wrath.

But still ...

Lochlan's AuzyAuzy Shiver, nicknamed the Golden Rush for the color of the great whites in the royal family, were formidable fighters. If by some stroke of bad luck the Indi mariners *were* beaten, Velenka had no doubt that someone would come looking to exact their own revenge on her. She had to shift the current somehow. It needed to be done delicately, of course.

Everyone was cheering, "Down with Lochlan and Gray!"

"Yes, yes, I am great," Finnivus said, nodding to the enthusiastic court. "And they will pay with their lives for daring to fight me!"

That was the opening Velenka was looking for!

"But Emperor Finnivus!" she yelled, loud enough to be heard over the others. "Please don't risk your own life by swimming with the armada! I'm sure Lochlan is a fierce enemy, but Gray is dangerous! He's devious and will stop at nothing to harm you if you leave your wonderful Indi homewaters!"

The royal court quieted into a murmur. Finnivus nodded, taking Velenka's false worry into consideration. She hoped that this idea would get inside the young emperor's head and cause him to stay. That way, she could also remain at court and not get into any sort of danger. Battles were unpredictable things. They sometimes turned on a fin flick. Better to avoid them altogether.

"Of course *we* fear nothing," Finnivus began. Members of the court shouted in full-throated agreement with the emperor. "Lochlan and Gray are indeed treacherous and vile. But perhaps we won't have to worry about them at all. Why, with any luck, neither of them will be around when we swim out—*tomorrow*! We will destroy every single fin in the entire Atlantis Ocean, scrubbing it clean of their traitorous filth! We so decree it, and so it shall be!" And with that Finnivus howled with laughter.

Velenka was thunderstruck. They were leaving tomorrow? This had to be something he'd just decided! A royal whim she could do nothing about! Velenka hadn't heard a thing about this—and she made sure to overhear every single conversation she could!

It was then that Velenka decided that a more direct plan would be needed to ensure her own safety, and so began doing what she did best . . .

Plotting.

CHAPTER 4

Gray rushed forward to press the attack using the Seahorse Circles, a tight turning move aimed at Lochlan's tail. The golden great white answered with Manta Ray Rising to foul the maneuver. The pair pounded each other with a series of rams and bumps, neither able to gain an advantage. "Nice one," Lochlan said through gritted teeth as he flashed forward. "But watch yourself! Don't over-commit when you're tired."

Gray smiled through his weariness and zipped to the side, avoiding the great white's lunge. They had been combat training for hours, and he ached from snout to tail. "Tired? Who's tired?" Gray wheezed. "I'm still gliding easy from my one-match winning streak against you."

"Now you're just being cocky, mate!" Lochlan tail-whipped Gray across the snout so hard, motes of color flashed before his eyes in the dark blue water. It was all he could do to execute Waving Greenie to stalemate Lochlan's lightning fast Tang Twist.

After another minute, Gray and Lochlan both got sloppy, neither able to finish their attacks crisply. Soon the one-on-one drill resembled a schoolyard fight more than the deadly dance they were striving to perfect.

"Stop, stop! I have seen turtle hatchlings battle with more grace!" Takiza yelled, shaking his frilly fins in annoyance. "This display of clumsy brawling hurts my eyes as I am forced to watch it!" The betta had appeared in the Riptide homewaters as suddenly as he had left, but refused to say where he had gone.

Gray and Lochlan hovered with the current in the training area, their gills opening and closing in short bursts as they struggled to catch their breaths.

"Aw, come on, Takiza, no one can keep up with us," Gray panted.

The little betta stared haughtily from his position above their heads. "What was that, Nulo? Did you once again embarrass yourself by speaking?"

Gray ducked his head and addressed Takiza by his honorific. "What I meant was, Shiro, that I think Lochlan and I are pretty good. Maybe you could say something nice to us every once in a while." Shiro was a word that meant *master* and *teacher*, while Nulo meant *student* and, according to Takiza, *nothing*.

"Now you've gone and done it," Lochlan whispered.

"You're on your own." The golden great white moved away as the betta gave Gray a steely gaze.

"Never have truer words been spoken, Nulo. You *think* you are good. Which is why you should never think!" Takiza zipped around, somehow creating some sort of disturbance with his gauzy fins and his mastery of Shar-kata, which caused Gray to tumble and roll in place. He was about to vomit up the fat haddock he'd eaten earlier when Takiza finally stopped. Gray listed to the side as he tried to regain a sense of which direction was up and down.

The betta fish appeared in front of his left eye. "When Nulos *think*, it only leads to trouble!"

Lochlan laughed. "That was fin-tastic, Takiza. Especially when it's not me!"

"Really, *fin*-tastic?" Gray asked.

Takiza regarded the golden great white. "Oh? You find my lesson humorous? Do I amuse you? Perhaps you are laughing at me?"

Lochlan stopped grinning at once. "Wait, now. I didn't say that, Takiza."

"I'm pretty sure he did, Shiro," Gray added immediately.

"Not helping." Lochlan retorted. "And I will get you for that."

Takiza swam closer, his billowing fins rippling with the slow tide. For a tiny Siamese fighting fish, he could strike fear into even the largest shark's heart. "Perhaps I was born into the Big Blue solely to be your court jester, King Lochlan. Indeed, perhaps I am no more than a clown fish, to flit through the water for your amusement. Please, tell me if this is so, and I shall begin flitting at once."

Lochlan bobbed his head deeply and more than once. "No, Shiro. What I meant to say is that you are wise beyond your years. Wise and also strikingly handsome. Have you lost weight? My overall point was that you should be commended for putting up with our many, many, almost uncountable, deficiencies."

Takiza looked at Gray and cracked the slightest of grins. "See? Wisdom. That is why he is the rightful King of the Sific."

Just then, Whalem came tearing through the water. The old tiger shark slid to a halt, panting heavily. He had refused all suggestions to go to the royal doctor fish for treatment, saying that nothing could change the currents of old age. "I've just received word from our advance scouts that the Black Wave is preparing to leave the Indi Ocean!"

"So it begins," Takiza said quietly.

"Did your scouts see the size of their force?" asked Lochlan, concern etching his face.

Whalem paused. "They will have more than two thousand mariners."

"Two thousand?!" Gray gasped. "Even if we get Hammer and Vortex Shivers to join with us, we'll barely have half that!"

"I can gather another hundred from the Sific," Lochlan said thoughtfully. "We'll still be down, but it's not hopeless."

"What of their leadership? Who is the mariner prime?" asked Takiza.

Whalem ground his teeth together in frustration, making an audible scraping noise. "I was hoping for a pup from their Line, but Finnivus has chosen well this time. He's promoted my best commander."

"So we can't count on him making mistakes," Lochlan muttered. "We *need* Grinder and Silversun's forces."

"Maybe we should swim away while we have the chance," Gray said, his stomach roiling with anxiety.

"Evil must be met and defeated," Takiza said, shaking his filmy fins.

"He's right, Gray," Lochlan added. "To swim and hide won't be an option."

Gray nodded. They would have to be ready. Finnivus and his Black Wave were coming to destroy them all.

"This is just nuts!" muttered Barkley as their formation wheeled and moved forward in the cold dark waters next to the Maw. Gray named it *Takiza's Torture Pit* after he'd been trained regularly there by the little betta.

Now it's our turn, Barkley thought. Stupid Striiker! He was doing this to act like a hard-shell drill instructor.

But they were getting better, Barkley had to admit. His big, hotheaded friend was actually *good* at this.

"Come on!" Striiker yelled after their formation's shape became disorganized. "I make one thing different, like this new depth, and you've all turned into crying sea cows! Is it because you're scared of the dark? Do I need to get mama to rub your flank and tell you a story? Do it again!"

Barkley longed to be back at Riptide. His first experience living there had been a horror. But that was under the bullying rule of Goblin and his Line. Now that Gray was in charge, Barkley found that he loved the Riptide homewaters. The ancient place with its colorful terraced greenie and wide open spaces felt homey and inviting. Sure, not as many dwellers swam there now that the impending doom of Finnivus's armada was coming to smash them, but Barkley still loved the place. He even found that he shared one thing with the now-deceased Goblin. He felt that the Riptide homewaters were worth defending. With their lives, if necessary.

Let's just hope it's not necessary, Barkley thought.

"What are you doing, dog-breath?" yelled Striiker, somehow right next to him.

"Umm, nothing?"

Stupid! I let my mind wander! Barkley yelled inside his head.

"Oh, it wasn't nothing, doggie!" roared the great white. "You were daydreaming!"

Barkley stammered, "I—umm—"

"That wasn't a question!" Striiker shouted in his ear, causing Barkley to wince. "I can tell you were dreamin' of a nice, fat fish for dinner. Of hovering in a warm, cozy current while you ate it! Tell me I'm wrong, doggie!"

He actually *had* been thinking of that earlier. Had Striiker developed some sort of mind-reading powers recently? No, no, I'm just woozy from the pressure in this place, he thought.

"What do you have to say for yourself, doggie?" In his capacity of drill instructor, Striiker insulted everyone, but Barkley thought that as a dog shark, or dogfish, he got a little extra. He tried not to take it personally, but this rankled. No one seemed to respect dogfish.

Wisely, Barkley didn't mouth off. The entire group had learned that if anyone said *anything*, Striiker would add another hour to their training. He stuck to his attention hover, eyes forward, mouth closed.

The great white grunted and swam to his position in front of the formation. "Okay, back to it! This time with feeling!"

The group roared, "Yes, sir!" and began shifting formation as Striiker called out the commands.

Barkley sighed. Only two hours to go.

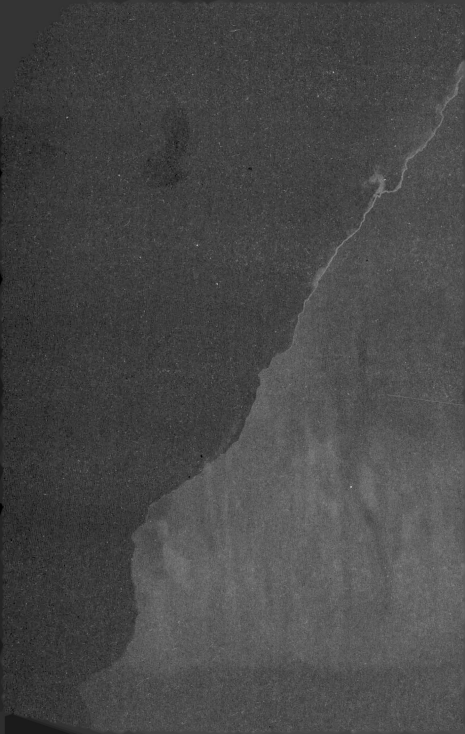

CHAPTER 5

GRAY GULPED DOWN HIS THIRD FISH OF the night. "You should try the sea trout with hot seasoning."

Lochlan had insisted that Gray take a night off to stop worrying about Finnivus. Of course Gray didn't want to. There had to be something to do to prepare. But after a while it was Mari who convinced him that nothing more could be done right now. If Finnivus was moving toward them, it would still take the Black Wave several weeks—even at top speed—to reach them. "And worrying about something that you can't do anything about is pointless," she told him.

The preparations for the invasion were in the capable fins of Lochlan, Whalem, Quickeyes, and many others. No matter how hard it was, Gray would relax tonight. He would get to spend some time with Mari, just the two of them.

But that was before Barkley overheard and invited himself along.

At first Gray thought that Barkley tagging along would be awkward but soon realized he was relieved to have his friend there. Although he would have liked to be alone with Mari, Gray realized he didn't know the first thing to say when that happened. With Barkley, there were no pauses in the conversation. The dogfish always had something to say.

The three of them gathered at Slaggernacks by one of the many flattened stones, which were the prime spots to eat and watch the musical entertainments. The seasoned fish was brought over by the dwellers, usually turtles or large crabs. The meals were "dumb" fish, not thinking ones. Good fins in the Big Blue all knew the rule: *Silver or brown, gulp it down. Fish of color, find another.*

Mari seemed to be enjoying her fish, a fat salmon. It was kind of an introductory meal that Slaggernacks served for those who hadn't tried seasoned fish. The meals were prepared by stuffing the fish with different types of greenie gathered from the Big Blue. Gray heard that some of their spices came from all the way on the other side of the world, traveling by migrating whales to get here. He wasn't certain that was true, but it sure made for a good story during the meal. And the fish were delicious.

"I don't see why catching regular fresh fish has gone out of style," Barkley put forth as he took another tentative bite of his own salmon.

"It hasn't. It's just different," Mari replied.

"I guess," Barkley said. "But it seems weird for a shark to *pay* for fish. I tell you, that Gafin must be some kind of genius."

When you came to Slaggernacks, you had to bring more than one fresh fish in payment for what you ate, usually three or four for every one ordered. Some fish were valued even higher, sometimes seven or eight to one. This way the place had a steady supply of fish and the dwellers who worked there didn't have to hunt and worry about where their next meal was coming from. Barkley was right, though. Gafin, the mysterious owner of Slaggernacks and also, supposedly, king of the urchins and poisonous dwellers, *was* a genius.

"Barkley, are you going to be grumpy all night, or only part of it?" Gray teased.

"No, no. It's great that we're out together, and I do like the music. I said right away I was good with coming here."

"Yes, *right* away," echoed Mari, giving Barkley a weird look. Hmm.

The band started up. Entertainment was another thing Slaggernacks provided to attract customers. They organized musical groups to play while the diners enjoyed their seasoned fish. Of course whales had been singing since Tyro created the Big Blue. They were the ones who taught everyone else how to do that. But now many different dwellers banded

41

together, which was how the word *band* came to mean a musical group. At first it was mostly older dwellers who found it hard to hunt for their meals and who formed bands. But now you would just as likely find much younger fins and dwellers doing the singing. And these days, since you could become famous, many weird dweller combinations had formed groups. Between the music and the food, the whole Slaggernacks scene combined into an odd and enjoyable experience.

And tonight the band was great. They called themselves Wild Current and had a whale and several huge sunfish singing, along with two dolphins providing back-up vocals with their clicks, razzes, and whistles. From their position in front of Slaggernacks's various caves and coves, the current brought their music right into the place. It was fantastic!

"Look who it is," said a gravelly voice. "Youse fins enjoying your night?"

Gray, his mouth full, turned as Trank the stonefish floated into view. If Gafin had a Line of replacement leaders like sharkkind did, Trank would be the first in his Line. Barkley and Mari weren't very fond of Trank, as poisonous dwellers like stonefish had a bad reputation in general. They were often accused of threatening other dwellers with their deadly toxins to get what they wanted.

"Just listening to the band and eating some fish," Gray answered.

"Have youse tried the volcano sauce? Hot, hot!"

"That's a little too much for me," Gray said. He had made the mistake of trying the lava sauce last week. It made his mouth feel like he'd eaten *actual* lava. He wouldn't be doing that again.

"Big fin like youse shouldn't be afraid of adding a little spice to your life," Trank replied.

"I'm surprised you have time to chat," Barkley said with a smile. "Aren't there any crimes you need to commit?"

Mari looked mortified. "There's no call for that, Barkley."

"Youse bet your life there isn't," Trank huffed. "And if youse insult me again in my place, youse *will* be betting your life."

"Don't you mean Gafin's place?" asked Barkley, genuinely curious.

Trank's fins circled a bit faster. "Yeah, yeah. That's what I mean. But insult me again—"

Gray interrupted before things escalated. "Hey, everyone calm down."

"I agree," added Mari. "Trank, this fish is delicious."

"Thanks," grunted Trank. "We have a new seasoner—cuttlefish named Bozenka. He's a wizard of flavor, that one."

"A *wizard* of flavor?" Barkley asked incredulously. "What the heck is a—"

"Hold on!" urged Trank. "Something's not right. Something's—"

Gray felt a jangling buzz through every nerve in his body. He rocketed toward the ceiling a split second before Barkley yelled, "LOOK OUT!"

Two makos appeared from nowhere and charged Gray, ignoring his friends in their single-minded rush at him. Instincts and lightning-quick reflexes saved him from being immediately sent to the Sparkle Blue. As it was, one mako barely missed his gills. Barkley managed to rise and jostle the second mako's tail, spoiling its strike on Gray's left pectoral fin.

Slaggernacks exploded into a riot, sharks and dwellers tearing off in every direction. "Flashnboomer! Flashnboomer!" yelled Trank as he disappeared into the sandy bottom of Slaggernacks. It must have been some prearranged signal because a number of blue ringed octos and lionfish were suddenly among them, stinging the makos with their deadly venoms. In the cramped space of the cavern, it was impossible to do any real defensive moves. That was probably why the pair chose to make their move here. But since the attackers hadn't caught Gray by total surprise, the two much smaller makos were now at a disadvantage.

Gray did a Bull Shark Rush at the closest shark, smashing him against a razor sharp coral wall. The second mako was distracted by the poisonous dwellers, particularly the lionfish that finned him in the soft of his gums as he opened his mouth to charge. Mari rammed that mako in the side, as did Barkley from above. The combined forces of the two blows knocked the attacking shark senseless, and the poisonous dwellers swarmed, stinging so many times that the mako jerked and spasmed.

"Gray!" shouted Mari. "Are you okay?"

Gray kept his bulk pressing against the shark he had trapped. "I think so. Check on the one I have here, Barkley!" His voice cracked a little from the adrenaline coursing through him. The dogfish ducked into the tight space between Gray and the ceiling.

"Move away," Barkley instructed.

Gray did and saw that the mako had been speared by pointed rods of coral in three different places, including through the gills. His coloring was odd; not black on top and white on the bottom like usual, but dark bluish *everywhere*. It was the very shade of the water that would make him almost invisible for this time of night. Because of the mako's injuries, though, he wasn't long for the Big Blue.

"Why did you do this?" Gray asked, almost shouting.

"I was hired," the shark said. "Nothing personal." Slowly, his coloring changed from its weird bluish all over to the regular mako hide with black on the top and white on the bottom.

"Did you see that?" Mari whispered in wonder. "How did he do that?"

The group looked over, and the other mako did the exact same thing as his gills stopped moving.

"Because," Trank said as he swam up from his hiding place. "He's an assassin."

"I thought you were in charge of those," Barkley said. When Trank gave him a look, the dogfish added, "I mean, *if* you were in charge of those."

The stonefish nodded. "If Gafin had assassins, they would be *dwellers*. There was a rumor of assassin shark-kind long ago, but I've never seen anything like this in my life. I do know it would be *verrry* expensive." He nodded at Gray. "In a way, youse should be flattered."

"Who sent you?" Barkley asked urgently as the mako's gills struggled to pump his last breaths. "You're dying, so you might as well tell us."

"You already know."

"Finnivus!" breathed Mari, nervously switching her tail back and forth.

"Well, it didn't work," Gray said to the dying shark. "You two are done!"

The mako worked his jaws back and forth, close to death. He spit up a gob of blood as the light faded from his eyes. "Who—who said there were only two of us?"

CHAPTER 6

GRAY STARED AT THE BODY OF THE MAKO assassin. For a moment he was shocked numb. Then he realized what the mako had meant—they were after Lochlan, too!

"Back to Riptide!" he shouted to Barkley and Mari as he roared from Slaggernacks. He was a good distance ahead of them on the high-speed swim to the homewaters, so he was the first to hear the commotion coming from there. A feeling cold as ice froze his insides, but he accelerated to an attacking sprint, leaving Barkley and Mari further behind.

"Look out! Here they come again!" shouted an Auzy-Auzy mariner.

"Where?" Gray shouted. "What direction?"

A squad of mariners charged him. They thought *he* was the attacker!

AuzyAuzy tiger shark Jaunt skidded in front of him.

"Ease off, you wonky drongos! Doncha see it's Gray? Swim the perimeter and look sharpish!" The AuzyAuzy sharks did as they were told.

"Jaunt, what happened?" Gray asked as Barkley and Mari joined them.

"There's been an attack against King Lochlan!"

Mari gasped. "Is he okay?"

"He has to be," Barkley said grimly.

Gray thought it was odd, the way his friend put that.

Jaunt nodded, but looked upset. "You should come with me."

She led them to one of the areas where Riptide mariners slept when they weren't on patrol. Gray's heart leapt when he saw the golden great white. He was alive! "Lochlan!" he yelled as relief washed over him.

But when the AuzyAuzy king turned, Gray could see he was injured. A ragged bite had been taken from his side. The doctor and surgeonfish were tending the wound, nibbling the edges that were now sutured together with urchin spines by the nimble claws of skillful crabs. AuzyAuzy Shiver was an ancient shiver, and its injury care was second to none. But this wound was deep.

The sight of Lochlan's injuries made Mari whisper a shaky, "Oh no . . ."

"These scratches? No worries." Lochlan shook his broad head dismissively. "It's nothing. But we lost two of my guards, and also—"

Barkley was aghast. "I know you're tough, but you've lost *part* of your flank."

"A sliver. I can swim fine. But I have to tell you three something—"

"Does anyone know if Coral Shiver was attacked? Are they safe?" Gray asked over Lochlan, who was distracted by another surgeonfish who came out of Goblin's old resting cave. This particular dweller Gray recognized as Oceania. She looked at Lochlan and shook her head sadly. Her reaction seemed to deflate both Lochlan and Jaunt.

"Your family is fine," Jaunt told Gray. "Let Loch finish."

Gray didn't listen. "I can't believe this happened in the middle of our homewaters!" he yelled, a bit louder than he wanted. "How can we defend against Finnivus if we can't even keep you safe?"

"Do you think you can still lead?" Barkley asked Lochlan.

"Stop asking dumb questions, Barkley!" shouted Mari.

"Quiet, everyone! Please, let me speak!" Lochlan ordered. Gray, Barkley, and Mari stopped talking. "I would be swimming the Sparkle Blue for sure—"

Gray knew he shouldn't be speaking—that Lochlan had something important to tell him—but he had a bad feeling and didn't want to hear it. He interrupted again, "But thankfully you're not and—"

Lochlan bumped Gray hard, repeating himself more

49

forcefully. "I would be swimming the Sparkle Blue for sure . . . if it weren't for your friend . . . Shell."

"Fought like a prehistore monster, that one. A finner of the highest order," Jaunt said in a cheerless whisper.

Gray shook his head from side to side, preventing the thought from settling in his mind. This couldn't be. This could *not* be!

"What are you saying, Lochlan?" Mari asked. But she already knew.

So did Barkley. "We've got to hear the words," the dogfish told him.

"Your friend Shell died saving me."

It was agreed that no good would come from letting the rest of Riptide United see Shell's body even though he was a hero. It was ripped and torn beyond belief, a grim reminder of what Finnivus wanted to do to everyone.

"Hard to believe he could keep fighting," Lochlan said in wonder as Mari cried silently nearby. Gray viewed the body of his friend with deep shock, but for some reason, tears did not come. He didn't feel anything, and that made him feel like a monster.

"They attacked without a whisper of warning," said Jaunt. Since Xander and Kendra, two other members of Lochlan's Line, weren't here—they were back in the Sific Ocean guarding the AuzyAuzy territory—Jaunt was in charge of Loch's personal safety. She was taking the attack badly. "Like a stupid puffer fish, I didn't see anything coming!"

"None o' that now," said Lochlan. He rubbed her flank with his tail. "It wasn't your fault. They were invisible!"

"If you had seen anything, *you* would have been killed first," said Takiza as he floated inside the cove where Shell's body and the bodies of two more mako killers lay. "What did you mean, they were invisible? They are visible now."

"But they weren't," Jaunt told Takiza. "Honest! It was like they blended in."

"So did the ones who attacked us," Gray said. "After they were . . . dealt with, they changed to a normal mako coloring."

"It's true." Mari nodded in agreement, hovering by Gray. She was trying to be brave, but he could taste her tears in the water.

"This is well and truly troubling," the betta muttered.

"Trank told us they were assassins," Barkley said.

Takiza rounded on Barkley. "They are not assassins!"

Everyone's mouth hung open. They'd never seen the serene betta show this much emotion. Takiza checked his anger and addressed the wide-eyed Barkley. "These are *fin'jaa*. The personal guard of the Seazarein. But she would never allow them to be used this way."

"Finja?" Barkley asked, using the more common pronunciation. "They're . . . *myths*."

51

Finja were ghost stories that mothers used to scare their pups when they misbehaved, very ancient ghost stories from prehistore times. "But everyone thought Takiza was a myth, too," Gray said.

"Okay, finja I can understand," Barkley gave in. "But the Seazarein? That position went away with the pre-histores."

Lochlan raised an eyebrow. "That's real, too?"

Takiza shook his frilly fins. "Do not become Nulo once again. Training you out of that period in your life was trying enough the first time."

"Father never mentioned anything about a Seazarein, and he was king of an ancient shiver. He would have told me if one was still swimming around, giving orders."

"The new Seazarein is not like that. She prefers to exercise her will in more invisible ways, unlike in ancient times."

"More invisible ways? Like assassinations?" asked Lochlan.

"Never!" said Takiza, chopping his fins through the water as if the matter was settled beyond a doubt.

Gray didn't know what was going on. Although he, Mari, and Barkley were all devastated by the loss of their friend, the dogfish's curiosity got the best of him.

"Can someone please tell me what a Seazarein is?" Barkley stared sadly at the unmoving body of Shell, only dimly visible in the dark cavern. "And why she maybe killed our friend?"

"She did not!" Takiza insisted. "She would not!"

"Lochlan? Please," Mari said. "The Seazarein." Gray motioned for Lochlan to take over while Takiza inspected the makos, muttering to himself.

"Seazarein is just a title, like King or Queen," Lochlan began. "But kings and queens would pay tribute to the Seazarein in ancient times. They served at his or her pleasure. The Seazarein was said to be the most powerful ruler in all the Big Blue. In charge of doing whatever was necessary to keep peace in all the wet-wet. If you became a tyrant, the Seazarein would send her *fin'jaa* to give you a warning. If a warning wasn't enough, well, that was it for you."

"So she's kind of like a secret emperor of the ocean?" asked Gray.

"Emperors and Empresses served the Seazarein in ancient times," Takiza said. "If she found a ruler who was so worthy that they could bring peace, the Seazarein would help them."

"You think that flipper Finnivus found out there was a Seazarein again?" asked Jaunt. "Tried to use her, maybe?"

It was a really good question.

Everyone, even Lochlan, looked at Takiza for an answer.

"Indi Shiver has always had an exceedingly high

opinion of itself. They would most likely consider the concept of Seazarein a myth, as it would diminish their own standing."

Lochlan looked at Takiza. "Indi *is* one of the ancient shivers. What if Finnivus not only knew about this new Seazarein but moved against her? What if he took control of the finja?"

The little betta fish didn't answer for a moment. Then he said, "Pray to Tyro that it is not so. But I must be sure!"

As everyone watched, Takiza swam away so swiftly he left a stream of bubbles in his wake.

CHAPTER 7

FINNIVUS WAS STILL RAGING SIX HOURS AFTER he had received word that his assassins were unsuccessful. "I was promised they *never* failed! I was *promised*!"

The emperor ripped off another piece of the royal herald who had the bad luck of having to deliver the message. She hadn't gotten another word out after, "I regret to inform his Magnificence that the *fin'jaa* have failed." Boom. That was it.

The armada had not moved a tail stroke since then. That was all right with Velenka. She had no desire to speed toward what was sure to be a bloody battle with Gray and his mariners. And their forces had been making good time. Too good! They were nearly by the southern tip of the African land mass. Soon, they would leave the Indi Ocean entirely and enter the Southern Atlantis.

"Tydal! Why did they fail?" Finnivus asked the cowering court shark. The epaulette had his snout in the sandy bottom of the court below the emperor's whale and the Speakers Rock embedded in its back. "Tell me why?"

"I would not presume to know, your Magnificence!" he whimpered.

"You are useless, Tydal! Useless!"

Fin'jaa. Velenka hadn't known such things existed until Finnivus had blurted out his plan this morning at breakfast. "Lochlan and Gray are probably already dead!" he'd crowed. But no matter how delicately Velenka tried to find out where the finja came from, or how Finnivus had found them, she was unsuccessful. Finnivus kept that secret to himself. And now, it seemed, these supposedly deadly assassins had not succeeded in dealing with Gray and Lochlan the way Finnivus had hoped.

Finnivus had gotten his hopes up far too high. Velenka's former shiver leader, Goblin, shared similar mood swings. But Goblin was a dim-witted fool compared to the emperor, and easily controllable. His moods changed often, but Velenka could shift them with little effort.

That was emphatically *not* true with Emperor Finnivus Victor Triumphant.

As if to prove her point, Finnivus shouted, "Guards, to me!"

Velenka tensed. The *squaline* darted into place from both above and below. The armored mariners formed a battle line so that anything threatening the Emperor would have to go through them. From what Velenka had seen, that would be nothing in the Big Blue. She doubted the landsharks above the chop-chop could find fighters more ferocious. The *squaline* were the best of the best. That was saying something as the Indi armada was the finest, most battle-ready force in the entire world. But even the *squaline* were not immune to the stormy moods of the emperor.

"No, no, no!" Finnivus yelled. "I didn't mean I was in danger! I want you to go out and find that—that lying finja and bring it to me immediately! *We* will wait here!"

The *squaline* flowed from their defensive positions into two perfectly matched lines. They didn't get more than five tail strokes before Finnivus shouted, "What are you doing? What if my enemies come? Who will guard me?" The *squaline* displayed no emotion as they resumed their normal guard patterns, one half swimming above the emperor and the other half hovering slightly below his mobile throne.

The blue whales switched positions, the second coming in underneath Finnivus as the first went for air. The third was away eating. The two here did the exchange so smoothly that the emperor rarely even noticed. But today wasn't a good day for anyone.

"What are you doing, you dolt!" Finnivus shouted for no reason and finned the blue whale's soft back, creating a scar. The blue whale didn't react, which was wise. There were many other scars from previous fits of temper, but whales were tough. Finnivus could spend an entire day biting before he reached something vital in a full-grown blue whale.

"Tydal, I'm hungry!" Finnivus wailed. "Bring me my supper!"

"Immediately, Magnificence!" The epaulette was gone in a flash. He was eager to be away from his place in court, and Velenka couldn't blame him. The emperor's temper was like a twisting current. You never knew which way the waters would churn, or who would be driven into the rocks.

"Stupid finja," Finnivus muttered like a pouty child. "That lying mako over-promised and under-delivered. Over-Promised Under-Delivered," Finnivus said, taking care to emphasize the first letter of each word. "O-P-U-D! Opud. I just made that up. It's brilliant!" Tydal returned and Finnivus told him, "Tydal, make sure my new word *opud* is used in daily conversation by everyone in court."

"Yes, my emperor!"

Finnivus preened for a moment and then gnashed his teeth once more. "But that's what he, she, or it is—an opud! And when I see that opudding dweller again, I'll—I mean, *we*—will have our vengeance!

Finnivus curled onto the mobile Speakers Rock on top of the blue whale and looked as if he were a minute away from a full-fledged weeping fit.

Opud! Incredible! It was hard to believe he was master of all he surveyed!

Velenka snorted.

She shouldn't have.

Finnivus whipped his head around, and his eyes locked onto her. Suddenly the tiger's body language was one of a dangerous predator. Very dangerous. "Yes?" he asked quietly.

She heard the question clearly as it was dead silent in the court. Velenka kept a bland smile on her face but knew well that her life hung by the slenderest of currents.

Dumb, dumb, dumb! Velenka yelled inside her mind. She had let her guard down, and the emperor's quicksilver mood had shifted, this time directly at her.

"You were saying?" Finnivus asked again, this time more forcefully.

Velenka couldn't ignore him any longer. She kept a neutral look, bobbed her head, and inquired, "I was saying what, my Emperor?"

"You chortled," Finnivus stated.

"Chortled at what?"

"How should I know? You were the one chortling!"

Velenka made sure to dip her head once more before she spoke. Ugh! She hated being so courteous to this fool! But bobbing her head was better than losing it! "If I did chortle—"

"YOU DID!" Finnivus screamed, startling some in the court so they twitched their tails. The emperor glared at them. Everyone looked guilty when they twitched. Velenka made sure she didn't.

"Then it must be so, My Magnificence," she answered. "I can only tell you I was so sad at your distress about those *opudding* finja that in my mind I was imagining Gray screaming as you shook him from side to side in your powerful jaws. If I did chortle, it was because of that image in my head, which I find especially pleasing."

Finnivus relaxed. He allowed the current to push him against the Speakers Rock on his blue whale's back. Then he addressed the court. "Do you see how effective my new word is? How radiant?" There were numerous murmurs of agreement. One of the other court sharks felt brave enough to tap Velenka on the flank in agreement.

"WHERE IS MY DINNER?!" Finnivus shouted. Tydal was off again, fast as a wahoo during a game of Tuna Roll. "And why are we stopped? I want Lochlan's head on a platter, so let's go!" The royal court and armada began moving once more toward the Atlantis and the final battle between Riptide and Indi Shivers.

But Velenka didn't care just now. Her time in the eye of Finnivus's stormy current was over, and she breathed a sigh of relief. She was almost ready to put her own plan into action. Velenka would get rid of the emperor and put herself on his throne. It would take some time, and, of course, her life would be at risk. But huge rewards only came with equally large risks. After all, Velenka was a descendant of Machiakelpi, the mako who was third in the Line of the First Shiver.

I'll just have to figure out a way to make his spirit proud, she thought.

CHAPTER 8

"SLOPPY, SLOPPY, SLOPPY!" STRIIKER BELLOWED at Riptide's recently recruited mariners. "Hold your positions until the order to attack is given! Watch and listen for the commands!" Striiker looked over at Whalem, who nodded approval. It took a lot of effort to swim around, correcting the recruits' mistakes, and the old tiger was in no shape to do that.

But Whalem could transfer his lifetime of knowledge and experience to Striiker in a series of one-on-one talks, as they had been doing since after the Battle of Riptide.

Barkley couldn't believe how well Striiker had learned everything. Whalem even taught Striiker the correct way of yelling to scare the recruits into listening closely. *Yelling* practice! Striiker was amazing. He soaked up every single word like a sea sponge. But it didn't give him the right to treat everyone like a loser.

Barkley couldn't take it anymore. He swam out from the massed formation and yelled, "We're trying our best! We aren't real mariners, so don't be such a tailbender!"

Striiker roared over and bumped him toward his place in the formation. "You're not a real mariner? Reality check—you better become a *real* mariner, even if you are just a *dogfish*, or your head will wind up on the emperor's platter! So excuse me if I don't have time to stroke your flanks and talk about hurt feelings!"

Barkley got back to his position, muttering something about great whites with big egos. Striiker heard and shouted, "What's that? What?"

"Nothing!" Barkley answered.

"Dog breath here just got everyone another hour of training!" Striiker announced. "Anybody else have something to add? Any of you? Then, fins up and attention hover!" There was much grumbling, but the group of newly drafted sharks snapped into position. The great white grunted, satisfied. "We're going to keep doing this until we get it right!" Striiker began the drill again. This time the result was somewhat better.

But Barkley was still irritated. Striiker never made fun of a tiger, or blue shark, or especially a great white, by insulting their entire *species*. But for Barkley it was always *doggie* this, or *dog-breath* that. Striiker—and many others—always had an extra insult about dogfish ready to go when they got into an argument with him.

Barkley stewed. I'll show him! So help me I will!

Unfortunately his mind wasn't on the drill and he turned the wrong way, causing a tremendous crash as sharkkind swerved to avoid ramming him. Soon, Striiker was yelling about dogfish in general—and him in particular—once more.

All Barkley could do was hover there in front of everyone and take it.

Lochlan spoke with Whalem quietly as Gray hovered with Grinder and Silversun in a private area by Speakers Rock in the Riptide homewaters. The two shiver leaders had agreed to make their decision on whether Hammer and Vortex Shivers would join with Riptide or not. In the distance Striiker was putting their mariners through a series of drills. Even from here, Gray could see it wasn't going well.

"More bad news, I'd say," muttered Grinder, gesturing with a fin toward Whalem.

"It might not be," Gray said, concentrating more on Silversun, who seemed by far the more reasonable fin of the two. "Let's wait and see."

"This thing is going sideways already," Grinder huffed.

Gray felt hot irritation rise in his throat and ground his teeth together to keep from saying anything. The more he got to know the Hammer Shiver leader, the more he wanted to tell him to stick his snout where the sun didn't shine.

Lochlan swam over after Whalem departed. "I'm not going to put a sunny glow on the news. Part of this meeting is so you know everything that we do." The Auzy-Auzy king paused and then told the group, "We've lost another entire patrol. Finnivus is picking them off, as we feared."

"Just great," growled Grinder. "The brat might even know we're here with you!"

"I doubt it worsens the danger we're in already," said Silversun. "Have you taken any precautions so it won't happen again?"

"Gray's going to find the best sharks for the job and get them trained into a special squad," the golden great white told them.

Gray nodded when Grinder and Silversun looked his way. Thankfully, even though this was the first he was hearing about this, he managed to say, "I just have to decide on the best fin for the job. It'll be soon, though."

"Better be. But improved scouts are the least of your worries," said Grinder. "I've seen your mariners. If it's not their first day of training, it's close."

Gray wanted to shout but Lochlan only nodded in agreement. "You're right about that, Grinder. That's why we'd like Hammer Shiver to join with us. Riptide United could certainly use the example of your fine mariners to be the best they can be."

"I know that," Grinder told Lochlan. "But our territory is far away, just like Vortex Shiver's. The holding force Indi left knows we're there and doesn't dare do anything because we'd rip them apart." Grinder clacked his serrated triangle teeth together for emphasis. "So why should we go to war with you?"

Silversun watched Lochlan intently for his answer. Gray sensed that the small port jackson shark was extremely intelligent and would be useful in the coming fight. Grinder, though, Gray could do without. But Lochlan said they needed every mariner they could get. The golden great white turned, his wounds making it difficult, and faced the muscular hammerhead leader. A faint trickle of blood oozed from the deep gash in his flank. The doctor and surgeonfish had sutured the wound three times now, and still, it bled. "So why haven't you driven them off?"

Grinder shook his fins in irritation. "Just waiting for the right time."

"If Finnivus destroys us, he'll point his snout at you next," said Lochlan. "Maybe not that day, or even the next month. But he *will* come."

"And we'll fight!"

"I know. But in the end, you'll lose. Just like we'll lose without you." Lochlan looked at both Grinder and Silversun. "Separately, each of us will lose *everything*. This evil cannot be hidden from, it cannot be bargained with, and we cannot swim far enough away. Finnivus is coming to destroy everything we hold dear. But together—together we have a chance. It's not a sure thing, but it's the best chance we have, mate."

Gray felt like cheering, but he was also chilled to his core. In just a few words, Lochlan had made the specter of Finnivus feel as if it were hovering next to them. The golden great white was a true king, and Gray would follow him into the Dark Blue if he asked.

But the stubborn hammerhead wasn't so easily convinced. "And who's going to lead us? You, slopping blood into the water every time you take a tail stroke? I can taste you from here. It doesn't inspire confidence."

Gray exploded. "Okay, chowderhead! How about I shut that cod hole of yours?!"

The hammerhead was more than ready for a fight, but Lochlan pushed between them. "Stop! Both of you, stop!"

Gray stared balefully at the hammerhead who gnashed his teeth in fury.

"What we're not here to do is fight each other," Lochlan continued urgently.

Grinder eyed Gray a little longer and then grumbled, "Fine."

Lochlan gestured pointedly with a fin at Gray. "And don't you have something to say?"

Gray dropped his tail, ashamed. "Grinder, I'm sorry. You're a shiver leader and deserve respect. I got angry."

Grinder nodded sharply. "Done." The hammerhead turned to Lochlan. "I know you're a king and a great leader. And my father's father told me he thought Auzy-Auzy Shiver was the paragon of all shivers, even as he fought against you. That was a stupid war, and I see this isn't. But the question still stands. You're in no shape to lead your forces into battle against the Indi armada. AuzyAuzy won't follow me because of our past, I know that. So, who will they follow? Because a fighting force needs someone out front and strong. They need someone to believe in."

Gray's eyes drifted toward Silversun. The brown and white shark chuckled and shook his head. "Oh, no. I can't swim an attack sprint with a raging current at my tail. Besides, as you might have guessed, we port jacksons aren't the fiercest fighters in the Big Blue."

"Yeah, Finnivus would laugh himself to death if you swam diamondhead," muttered Grinder to himself, but everyone heard. The diamondhead was the lead position in the center of a massed formation. The fin who gave the orders. Grinder didn't say it as an insult. He said it more in the realization their situation was dire. The hammerhead said it like they were facing the danger *together*. Gray was amazed. Lochlan had done it. Grinder was now on their side.

The hammerhead then realized just how insulting the comment was and turned apologetically to Silversun. "Oh, that didn't come out very—I—I—wow. There's no way to make that better, is there? Umm, whoops. Again, sorry."

To see the always puffed up and irritated hammerhead twitch his fins in total embarrassment made everyone burst out in gales of laughter. They howled so loudly that it took a moment for them to get control of themselves.

"Your question is a good one," Lochlan said when he was able to speak again. "It just so happens the leader of the AuzyAuzy mariners is right here."

It was a second before Gray noticed everyone was looking at him. "Me?"

"Him?" echoed Grinder.

"He has the look of a commander," remarked Silversun.

Lochlan kept going so Grinder couldn't get a word in edgewise. "Gray was the one who led the key attack that won the Battle of Riptide. He swam the diamondhead for us and swam it well."

Grinder nodded. "I heard. But he was there for one charge. Then you took over."

"*After* the Indi armada was smashed and scattered," Lochlan pressed. "Look, I know I'm injured. But with our dolph signaling system, I can still lead. If you don't think so, Gray *can* take over. He knows our system, and my Line respects him, as does everyone in Riptide."

"But you think you'll be there?" Grinder asked hopefully.

"Our scouts say Indi's main forces are two weeks away, so I *will* be ready," the golden great white answered. "But if you don't think I'm able, Gray will do it."

Grinder thought, then nodded. "I'll send for the rest of my mariners."

After the hammerhead swam off, Silversun bobbed his head in respect. "Well played, Lochlan. I'm with you also." As he left, the Vortex leader added with a grin, "But you already knew that."

When both sharks were out of earshot, Lochlan swirled his tail through the water victoriously. "Got 'em! Got 'em both!"

"That was great!" Gray said. "I can't believe you said all that stuff about me leading!" Gray imitated Lochlan's earnest speech. "'If you don't think I'm able, Gray will do it.' What a load of chowder!"

"Oh, that wasn't chowder, mate," Lochlan said. "Grinder's right. There's no way I can swim diamond-head. Let's start teaching you how to direct a massed for-mation! Exciting, huh?" The great white slapped Gray's flank as he passed.

"Wait, hold up," Gray pleaded, stunned. "You're not serious! Loch? Loch!"

CHAPTER 9

IT TURNED OUT THAT LOCHLAN WAS VERY serious. Gray spent most of the next three days practicing with the core of the AuzyAuzy force, half their mariners taking the place of Riptide United (which would now include Hammer and Vortex Shivers) with another group pretending to be the opposing Indi armada sharks. They trained east of the old Riptide and Razor Shiver territories. The rocky area wasn't good for hunting, so hardly anyone went there, which was ideal for their purposes. Lochlan didn't want anyone to see Gray practicing so hard and he certainly didn't want Grinder and Silversun having any second thoughts about joining Riptide United.

And wow, did they train.

The pace was fevered. Everyone knew that Finnivus and his mariners were swimming ever closer, tail stroke by tail stroke. The Black Wave was coming, and they had to be ready.

"Tripletail Turns Down, execute!" yelled Gray. Olph, the lead dolphin swimming in close order above his dorsal fin, click-razzed the commands. Their formation lurched downward as if it were a single fish.

Gray had met "Olph the battle dolph" after the Battle of Riptide. His family had been battle dolphs with Auzy-Auzy Shiver for centuries. To work with Olph, Gray had to take a crash course in the dolphin language, which was maddeningly hard to follow. But their clicks, whistles, and razzes would cut through the noise of a battle, when yelling wouldn't.

Gray was surprised to learn that dolphins had several dialects. Click-razz was the quickest (which is why it was an excellent signaling system), whistle-click-razz was what dolphs normally spoke with each other, and whistle-click was the slower, more elegant version of their language used for formal occasions. Gray didn't care about this newfound knowledge at the moment. He was blundering right and left, and one of the reasons for this was that Olph the battle dolph was swimming so close to his topside that it seemed like he was *glued* to Gray's dorsal fin. But Lochlan wasn't making allowances for distractions.

"Don't *yell* 'execute' unless you have to!" the AuzyAuzy leader shouted from the side. "It slows you down! You were swimming level and could have used a fin signal."

"What if Olph misses it?"

The dolphin made a grating series of razzing noises.

Gray didn't understand a word, but he could sense it wasn't a compliment.

Lochlan shook his head in an exaggerated way. "Olph *never* misses! Now, continue, my young Nulo—"

"Do *not* even start with that!" Gray shot back.

"The enemy has reformed and outnumbers you two to one," the golden great white said in a strong voice. "They close with Grouper Dances Through the Greenie before attacking with a Tang Twist! Now!"

The opposing formation did the maneuvers and rushed at Gray's forces.

"Umm, uh, Snapper Skims the Seabed!" Their own formation went even lower. "Manta Ray Rising!" Olph clicked out a signal immediately. The rest of the mariners followed Gray as if they were part of his own body. Sometimes, when they got it right and the hundreds of sharks around him whooshed a turn totally in sync, leading from the diamondhead was absolutely thrilling. Unfortunately, those bits of wonder were few and far between.

"Spinner Strikes!" Gray called out.

When used in single combat, the Spinner Strikes was an attack from below aimed at a shark's soft underbelly. If successful, it was almost always fatal. Gray remembered too late that it wasn't very good for *massed* fighting, though. The opposing force fell on them with the ferocity of a flashnboomer, crushing their formation using Orca Bears Down.

"Oh, come on, mate!" yelled Lochlan, irritation showing. "You can't make that mistake!" Lochlan flexed his fins and winced. His injured side was oozing blood again and clearly bothering him. "Sorry. Let's take a break."

"I understand why you're disappointed," Gray told him when they were off to the side. "I wouldn't want me leading your friends, either."

"You'll get the hang of it," Lochlan said with a weak grin. "And I'll be there just in case. No worries."

"You know, I have an idea!" Gray said, getting the golden great white's attention before he swam away. "Dolphins give you a big advantage, don't they?"

"Well sure, that's why we use them, especially Olph. He's magic, you'll see."

"But my point is, what about other dwellers? How about whales?"

Lochlan shook his snout from side to side. "Whales are defenseless in a fight. Too slow, and they don't like to scrumble in general. Big enough to be pacifists, though, and that's why they aren't lunch. Most of the time."

"All whales are like that?" Gray asked, surprised. "What about those Arktik ones, the orcas?"

"They're actually cousins of Olph and his kin, not whales. But there are very few of them, and they live far away—"

Gray interrupted, "We could swim there and convince them! We'll get some maredsoo from Takiza to speed us along, and be back in no time." Maredsoo was a mysterious glowing greenie that grew in the Dark Blue, deep in the ocean. Eating a little gave you huge amounts of energy for long swims or even fighting. It was demon hard to get, though.

Lochlan shook his snout again. "Gray, the orcas swore to never take a side after the Battle of Silander's End. That's a long story and I'm tired. Just know that they will not join us. Especially in the time we have, which needs to be spent training you. Finnivus is on his way, so you need to *accept* the fact you're the one who will be *leading* our forces!" Lochlan yelled the last part, getting the attention of both Mari and Jaunt.

Mari shook her head at Lochlan as Gray's tail drooped. The great white was embarrassed. "You know what? We've done enough for today, and I'm getting cranky and tired. You'll get the hang of it. Mari, Jaunt, talk with him."

Lochlan swam off, probably toward his personal doctor fish to be patched up once more. The mariners training with Gray drifted off. Oh, the AuzyAuzy fins said nice things, but he could see it in their eyes that they were unsure. Truth be told, he was unsure.

"Howareya doin', ya big beauty?" asked Jaunt in her odd, lilting accent. The way the little tiger spoke always made Gray smile. She was infectious. "Quit hanging your head like a squiddily-kelpie. You'll be fine."

Gray shook his head. "I'm no squiddily-kelpie, Jaunt," he said, trying to lighten his mood. "You're a squiddily-kelpie!" When they first met, Jaunt had used the word *squiddily-kelpie*, and he hadn't had the slightest idea what it meant. Now, it was a joke between them. But she still wouldn't tell him what it was.

Mari smiled and cut her long thresher tail through the water. "You two come from the same reef in the boonie-greenie? I can barely understand either of you!"

Jaunt gave Mari a snout bump on the flank as they both laughed. "Oh, Mari, you wish you could speak extra special like Gray and me! Instead you chibber-chabber like every other biter in the wet-wet."

Gray chuckled, even though he didn't feel like it. He could tell this little show was to lift his spirits. But it wasn't working. "Jaunt, you're Loch's fifth. Why can't you take over and lead the mariners?"

"Because Loch wants you to do it, and I think that's right," she told him. "Besides, AuzyAuzy is a royal shiver. The Golden Rush have rules on who can take over."

"That's dumb!" he answered, slashing his tail through the water.

"Gray, you already did it once," Mari said. "I know you think you got lucky, but the fact is, you did it."

"There was no time to think then!" Gray's tail drooped. "I don't know if I can do this."

"Yes, you can," Mari disagreed. "But not with that attitude."

"You have the knowing," Jaunt told Gray. "You're a

little nervous today. But those belly crabs go away right quick with a little experience, and that's why Loch's training you up."

Gray sighed, exasperated. "Yes, Jaunt, my belly crabs will disappear after the *Indi armada* gets here! Oh, and I was so worried. But at least my belly crabs won't bother me as Finnivus's mariners are taking fins and tails from everyone I know!"

"Ya don't have to be such a drongo about it!" she yelled back.

Gray was past his limit. "WHAT DOES THAT EVEN MEAN?!" he shouted in her face before swimming away.

He knew he had hurt Jaunt's feelings, but right now, he didn't care. This was crazy! He wasn't cut out to be a leader of a real shiver, much less a battle shiver! Sure, he led Rogue Shiver, but they were all friends. And there were only six of them, total. But to be in charge of the safety of a thousand sharks, all their pups, the rest of the shiver sharkkind, and the dwellers that lived in Riptide's territory—that was too much!

"We need someone else!" Gray shouted into the water to no one. Could Takiza lead the armada? Would he even be there for the fight? Who could tell with the mysterious betta? But they needed someone else.

"Or something else," Gray muttered to himself in a much quieter voice. He kept saying it out loud. "Something else, something else, some-*thing* else ..."

That's it!

He knew what to do. Takiza probably wouldn't like it, but Gray was desperate. And what the little betta didn't know wouldn't make him mad.

Most likely, anyway.

Barkley saw Gray zooming from another secret training session. He had been hovering unseen in the tall greenie for just this opportunity. "Hey Gray!" Barkley said when he was right above him.

"*Gah!*" Gray shouted, startled. "What are you doing sneaking up on me like that?"

"Umm, sorry," Barkley said. "I'm sneaky, remember? I need to talk with you for a minute."

"I don't have a minute!" his friend snapped.

Barkley kept pace. He was speedy for a dogfish. "Look, I want to be helpful, but being in the armada—"

Gray wheeled, and Barkley banged his snout against his rock-like side. "What? Are you too good to fight?"

"Of course I'm not too *good* to fight!" Barkley protested. "I'm too *bad* to fight!"

"Let me tell you something," Gray shouted. "We all wish we could do something else, especially me! But sometimes you have to swim with the current that's flowing!" And with a flick of his powerful tail, Gray was gone.

The pressure was really getting to his friend. And Lochlan didn't seem to be getting any better. We're in real trouble, Barkley thought as he swam through what used to be the Razor Shiver homewaters.

The fact remained, he was a terrible mariner.

If there was only something else I could do!

Barkley had tried being a long-range scout but discovered he wasn't strong enough. A dogfish didn't have the endurance to swim the distances in the time necessary to bring in vital information. Blues and tigers were much more suited for that. And every fin was needed in the armada. If Riptide United's formation was too much smaller than its foe, the Indi armada would simply overwhelm them.

So, my job is to be chum, Barkley thought. The best I can hope for is that a Black Wave mariner chokes on me. I'm worthless.

"Move aside, doggie!" said a group of Hammer Shiver mariners as they swept past. The last one gave Barkley a tail slap to the face and they all laughed.

Barkley thought most big mariners were chowderheads. They never had to swim away from a threat when they were growing up. Many of the best ones were bullies from time to time. Or always. They certainly didn't show respect to anyone who couldn't hold their own in a snout-to-snout fight.

And of course, they don't have a high opinion of dogfish in particular, Barkley thought. Not many sharkkind do.

They were right in a way, though. They were mariners of Riptide United. They would be fighting on the front lines. They were risking their lives to protect every-one else. They were *useful*.

Barkley's tail drooped. He felt an electric charge tingle his left flank. Prime Minister Shocks was speaking to a group of refugees with Sandy by his side. Remnants of shivers attacked by Finnivus had sporadically arrived since the Battle of Riptide. But for some reason, even though the threat of Finnivus was coming closer, the numbers were growing. More and more came. And it wasn't as if Lochlan or any-one was keeping it a secret. They told everyone that the Riptide homewaters would be attacked as sure as the tide moves. Oddly, most decided to stay in spite of this.

Perhaps they were tired of moving, or perhaps they wanted revenge, although he didn't think the latter was the case. Barkley thought it was because Riptide was the one place in the Big Blue that offered hope. Here gathered the fins who refused to lower their snouts to that royal flipper, sharks who had actually swum out against Finnivus and bloodied his invincible armada.

Barkley let out an involuntary shiver. If they saw how he'd messed up during Striiker's practice drills, perhaps they'd think again. But still, they came.

This new group of refugees was a small one. Bar-kley wondered how big their shiver had been before they were attacked. He swam over and heard Shocks saying, "I know you have questions, but I don't have time to answer them now. Why don't you go feed? Follow Sandy. You look like you can all use a meal! While you do that, I'll find you a place to call your own." Shocks waved them away with his supple eel body.

The sharkkind refugees reluctantly moved off. Barkley could see many wore markings and tattoos, like Indi Shiver, but different. The group seemed confused at which way to go, and some were injured.

"Barkley, would you mind helping me out?" Sandy asked. She motioned that another group of refugees was coming. "Can you show them where to hunt and maybe talk to them while I help the ones coming now?"

"Sure," he answered, feeling a sense of relief. Here was something he could actually do.

Gray always says I never stop talking, Barkley thought as he waved the mixed group over. A few of these sharkkind had green stripes on their flanks. Another half-dozen had a triangular pattern on their bellies, and one older female had an orange dot on her tail.

"Hi, I'm Barkley!" he told them. "Why don't I take you to the hunting grounds?"

Everyone was grateful. They had been swimming

for weeks. Who knew when they had last eaten? But Barkley saw that the older shark with the orange dot on her tail didn't react as enthusiastically as the others. He hung back and swam beside her.

"Are you okay?" he asked.

She had been crying. "I'm fine," she answered, but she obviously wasn't. "Have you seen any others from my shiver?" She waggled her tail with its distinctive orange dot marking.

"Yes, I think so," Barkley said cautiously, and she brightened immediately. He knew that at least two of her shiver were here or he wouldn't have dared mention it.

She came closer to him, full of eager hope. "Are they—the ones from my shiver—are they pups, or adults?"

"Why, they're adults," Barkley answered. It was odd, now that he thought about it. Aside from the pups in Coral, there weren't too many from the refugee shivers. Looking at the two newest groups, he noted there were no younglings among them, either. "Why do you ask?"

The old shark grew sad once more. "Because after they attacked us, they took our pups." She began crying and rubbed against Barkley. "They took our pups!" she wailed.

Barkley tried to comfort her as best he could, but inside, his heart turned to stone.

He would help Riptide United beat Finnivus in whatever way he could.

And if the only way is to choke one of their mariners by swimming straight down its gullet, than that's what I'll do, Barkley thought.

CHAPTER 10

IT WAS EARLY MORNING BY THE TIME GRAY reached the deep-water coral fields where Striiker had been training the Riptide recruits a few days before. He was well-familiar with the area.

Takiza's Torture Pit.

The razor sharp coral spires were still there, standing silently in the dark waters. But Gray didn't have the same difficulty breathing he once did.

Must be Takiza's doing, he thought. The Siamese fighting fish had worked him mercilessly at these depths since the Battle of Riptide.

But a chill crept down Gray's spine as he drifted over the edge of the training field and saw the dark hole in the ocean called the Maw. That was where he could get the some*thing* that might give them the advantage they would need in the fight against Finnivus and his Indi armada—maredsoo!

It was Takiza who had told Gray that maredsoo only grew in the deep waters of the Maw, before sending him after some when they were about to face Finnivus and the Indi armada the first time. Takiza then swam across the ocean into the Sific and gave it to the AuzyAuzy mariners, so they could power back in time for the Battle of Riptide. Without that maredsoo, the Golden Rush wouldn't have made it, and everyone Gray knew would have gone to the Sparkle Blue.

Well, if it worked once, it could make the difference again!

Of course last time Takiza had woven Gray a greenie harness that held a rock, which dragged him downward. Now, he would have to power himself. Takiza had also gotten two devilfish to guide Gray. Now, he would need to find his own way.

Oh, come on, it's straight down, Gray thought. It doesn't get any simpler! Don't be a baby turtle!

It was well known that turtle hatchlings were the least brave dwellers in the entire Big Blue, and he definitely wasn't one of those. Yet Gray shivered as he felt the cold water rush past him on its way down into the blackness. It gave him the chills something fierce.

The Maw was so deep, it went into what sharkkind called the Dark Blue. Regular sharks didn't live there. Regular *dwellers* didn't live there. Everything that swam in the Dark Blue, at least those that Gray saw when he went down the first time, was weird and scary.

"You don't bother them, they won't bother you," Gray said to himself, trying to ease his fright. He hovered over the edge and yelled into the dark, "I'm not looking for any trouble. Just getting some maredsoo and then leaving."

No one answered, of course. The only sound Gray could hear was the heavy, black water whisking past his flanks. "Good, then," he announced, as if someone had answered that it was okay.

There was no sense in putting it off any longer. Here we go, Gray thought as he pushed himself over the ledge into the Maw. He pointed his snout straight into the deep blackness.

Going down.

Gray had timed his journey so it would begin when the sun was straight up above the chop-chop. But soon enough, there was only total darkness.

Gray kept his wits about him, concentrating on the currents and making sure he swam a straight course. If he didn't reach the bottom, it would all be for nothing.

Down, down, down, he went.

Gray panted heavily, his gills pumping the thicker, freezing waters into his body. It hurt. And the cold water made his body ache more than he remembered.

"I c-c-can do this," Gray told himself, teeth chattering. "I c-c-can do—"

BOOM!

Gray saw stars!

But there can't be stars! I'm nowhere near the sky, he thought. Then the tiny motes of light disappeared, leaving only pitch-blackness. Gray swam forward and *hit* something. He tapped at it with his tail, then rubbed a fin against it.

A rock.

What is a rock doing in the middle of the Maw? Gray puzzled. At least he wasn't cold. In fact, it was pretty warm, which was nice, but now he couldn't think straight. Everything seemed kind of fuzzy, like when the warm waters of the Caribbi Sea where he grew up had a mass of plankton float by. Maybe he should just relax and take a nap until his head cleared . . .

Wait a second!

Gray shook his snout from side to side, clearing it. He couldn't go to sleep in the Maw! What was he think-ing? Gray tried to move forward and discovered it wasn't a rock in the middle of the Maw. It was the *mountain wall* of the Maw!

Sometime during his descent Gray had turned *side-ways*! But when? For how far? And in which direction? Since he hit his head, Gray couldn't remember. And everything was dark around him.

"You look losssst, friend," said a hissing voice.

Gray tried to move away but hit the mountain wall again! "Who's that?" he asked, hoping his voice didn't crack too much.

"They call me Mog," the voice answered. "Jussst hold sssstill."

Gray might be dumb every now and again—like when I started swimming down here, he thought—but he wasn't *that* stupid. He rocketed away from where he thought the unseen voice was coming from. It was then that Gray felt the thickest, ropiest greenie ever, wrapping onto his flank. He adjusted his course, but the greenie stuck to his side.

Then a light flared!

It was a small light, not even that bright, but in the total blackness around him it was like a flashnboomer had gone off! Gray saw that what he *thought* was thick greenie wasn't greenie at all.

It was a giant octopus's tentacle!

There were voices speaking, but his concentration was totally on the monster attached to him. The ugly head seemed larger than Gray himself. Its beaky mouth screeched, a sound that chilled his blood. And the huge octo's other creepy, super-long, and very thick arms were coming for him, too!

The light went out when someone screamed in terror.

Is that high-pitched screaming coming from me? Gray thought woozily.

He churned his tail back and forth but didn't feel he was moving. He spun around and saw the huge octo holding onto his side. Gray was dragging it! He had to get this deep-sea horror off or else the giant Maw dweller would have him for lunch.

As if reading his mind, the creature growled in a raspy voice, "Sssstay sssstilllll!"

Two more voices started talking! "What's his name again?" asked one.

The other, more irritated, answered, "I don't remember. Big dumb fin? Chunky pup? Something like that?"

Gray felt himself being dragged closer to the immense octopus. He was about to give in to complete terror when he remembered something Takiza had told him: A clear mind is your best weapon.

Gray stopped struggling and let the cold waters wash over him.

Then, he knew.

If he were dragging the immense octo, swimming away would tire him out. He needed to attack and get it to detach. Gray turned and streaked at the Maw dweller, whose giant eyes—each the size of a fully inflated giant puffer fish—blinked in surprise.

BAMMO! Gray rammed the octo in its big, fat head, driving it down into the darkness.

"Ouuuuch!" it yelped.

That was kind of odd. Not really the reaction a Maw monster should have, Gray thought. He heard the other voices again, but now they were closer.

Another light pierced the darkness around him.

Gray found a devilfish floating by his eye. The little

horror's mouth bristled with long needle teeth, and its black, slimy skin glistened in its light.

"I hope you're happy! Now Mog is going to have a lump!"

A smaller devilfish, attached to the larger one's side with his fangs, said, "I can see why Takiza doesn't take you anywhere!"

As if through a haze, their names floated into Gray's mind. "Briny? Hank?" he asked, not sure if it could be true.

"See?" said Briny, the larger of the two. "He's coming around. I told you he didn't do it on purpose!"

"Do what?" asked Gray.

The smaller, male devilfish moved from his position on Briny's side. "First you blast through our party without even a hello. Then you smash your head on the wall, and when we send Mog to *show* you which way is up, you try and jerk one of his tentacles off. And you top it off by *attacking* him. I'm curious, I really am—where were you raised?" Hank then asked Briny, "I mean, really, who does that?"

Gray shook off his pain and weariness. The giant octo was closer and favoring the one tentacle. "It hurrrrtssss," he rasped.

Gray felt awful. It sounded like Mog was *crying.* "I'm so sorry," he said. "I thought you were trying to eat me."

"You're a sssstupid jerrrrrk," Mog replied. He was definitely sniffling. Could the giant octo be a *pup*? Unbelievable!

Gray's throat grew tight, but not because of the water. I've done something stupid! *Again!* he thought. And he was no closer to finding a way to save his friends from Finnivus and his mariners.

Briny swam closer, concern etched on her horrible, fang-filled, but somehow still kind features. "What's the matter?" she asked. She turned toward Hank. "Something's the matter."

"I'll tell you what's the matter," Hank grumbled. "He's a jellyheaded party ruiner. That's what's the matter."

"You shush," Briny told her husband. "Gray, tell me what's got you upset. You tell Aunt Briny this instant!"

So he did.

Gray told Briny, Hank, and even Mog—who had stopped sniffling and seemed to regain the use of his injured tentacle—about everything that was happening in the waters above: Finnivus, the finja, the armada, the death of Shell, how Takiza had gone who knew where, Lochlan's injury, and how Gray was expected to lead everyone to victory over the Indi armada! He ended with, "And I just don't think I can do it! I'm going to fail, and everyone I care about will swim the Sparkle Blue!"

"You poor boy," Briny said.

"Sssooo ssssad," Mog agreed, and then placed one of his huge tentacles gently over Gray's flanks. It didn't feel so bad, once you got used to it.

Kind of comforting, in fact.

"Hank, say something nice," Briny ordered.

"You care for your friends, so you're not a total loser," Hank said. "Let's get you back where you belong before you catch your death."

Gray was so tired from the swim that he knew there was no point in going deeper for the maredsoo. He would never make it. He let Hank and Briny guide him upward.

The depths, physical strain, and terror made him numb. Though Briny said many encouraging things, all Gray could focus on were Hank's words *before you catch your death*. The phrase echoed in his ears, and the blackness of the Maw seeped into his mind and darkened it.

When Gray got to the training fields, he swam home. He went fast, the time spent on his failed quest making his face burn with shame.

Finnivus is coming, and all I did was waste time! he chastised himself.

Gray felt like crying.

There is no hope, he thought. I *will* catch my death. Everyone will . . .

CHAPTER 11

IT HAD BEEN ONLY A DAY SINCE GRAY'S ill-fated trip to the Maw, and he was exhausted. But Whalem's scouts reported there was still time before Finnivus and his hordes arrived, so Gray carefully brought up the idea to get maredsoo for the mariners to Takiza, without actually saying he had already tried, of course.

It didn't go well.

The betta basically called him an idiot in his wordy way. He explained between insults that while maredsoo was good for giving energy for long-distance swims, it wasn't good in the short term. In fact, giving mariners maredsoo would guarantee they wouldn't be able to swim in battle formation. "They would have too much energy to concentrate on their orders, and half of them would be throwing up. But why do you ask such a stupid question?"

Gray quickly changed the subject and swam off to his training with Lochlan. Between Takiza and Lochlan, it was like he was being buffeted by two completely different, but equally rough, currents.

Yet the great white's golden color, so deep and healthy before, was now grayish and lacked its usual shine. Was Lochlan dying? Gray couldn't bear to think about that.

"Finally!" Lochlan shouted as Gray successfully completed a difficult series of moves capped by Spearfisher Streaks by the Cliffs with a large portion of AuzyAuzy mariners. "Not bad at all!"

"Not bad?" Jaunt said loudly. "That was bloody perfect."

Gray chuckled, relief apparent in his voice. "Guess I'm finally getting the hang of it!"

Just then Olph the dolph released a rapid series of clicks and whistles. Gray caught a word or two, but didn't understand all of what was being said. The Auzy-Auzy mariners who did hear began talking urgently among themselves.

Lochlan's eyes widened in surprise. "That can't be," he said.

Olph released a single loud click again, and the great white was silent for a moment.

"Jaunt, Mari, form everyone up."

Both sharkkind disappeared in a flash. A bad feeling crept into Gray's stomach as Lochlan told him, "That's all we have time for, mate."

"What?" asked Gray. "What do you mean 'that's all we have time for'? You mean for today, right?"

"They're here. Somehow, Finnivus's mariners are here."

"No, no, no!" Gray repeated, shaking his head from side to side. "I was there for the report this morning and we most definitely heard that they were far away!"

"And now I'm telling you they're here," Loch answered, gesturing for him to follow.

Gray felt a rising fear that paralyzed his body. He couldn't swim. His tail didn't work. Instead, he grinned at Lochlan. "Is this a joke? It's a joke, right? To see how I'll do under pressure. Very funny!" Gray cackled, but Lochaln didn't join in and the panicky feeling raced up and down his spine in hot flashes.

The golden great white gave him a steely gaze. "Okay, you've had your moment to freak out. But it's over, Gray. You hear me? It's over."

Gray's voice cracked. "This can't be happening, Loch! They're far away! The scouts—"

Lochlan was amazingly calm. How could he be so composed? "The scouts missed something, Gray. Olph heard it from one of the other dolphs. Their senses are even more fine-tuned than ours. We still have some time left. Our fastest fin just got here with this news, so we can get into proper formation and meet Indi snout to snout and at the ready. But if you want to do anything special before the battle, now's the time."

Gray immediately threw up.

"Not what I meant, but okay," said Lochlan. "Come on, big fella. Let's get going."

"Oh-okay," was all Gray could muster. He wanted to tell Lochlan that today was no good. Maybe they could postpone the battle until next week?

But Gray knew that there was no rescheduling.

Finnivus was here.

"Tyro help me," he whispered as Lochlan led him toward the Riptide training fields, which were literally vibrating with motion and emotion. Every sharkkind in their forces was rushing to get to their positions. The water would arc electricity if it got any tenser.

"Okay, I want to see even spacing above, below, and side to side!" bellowed Striiker to the Riptide mariners as they adjusted their section of a standard pyramid formation.

AuzyAuzy Shiver would form the center of the formation, Riptide taking position behind their mariners. It was the most protected position for the new mariners as they were still the least experienced, but they could counterattack from there. The experienced Hammer and Vortex Shivers hovered at the ready on either side and would guard everyone's flanks.

Lochlan waved Gray over to where he was talking with Grinder, Silversun, and Quickeyes. The golden great white swam out and spoke low. "Look, this was sooner than we expected. Maybe Finnivus split his forces; it doesn't matter. Just be confident. Our fins want to feel good about you."

I'm not feeling good about me, Gray wanted to say. But he didn't.

"How you doing?" asked Grinder. The brown and blue hammerhead twitched his large, pointed dorsal fin, nerves from the upcoming battle sparking from him.

"I feel fine," Gray said woodenly.

Lochlan gave him a stinging slap on the underbelly. "'Course he's fine! Better than fine!" Gray could see the look on Lochlan's face. You need more fire in your eyes, it said.

"Right!" Gray exclaimed forcefully. "Time to end this threat!"

"Good, then," Quickeyes added. "I like our new home-waters and don't want to leave." Quickeyes had only left a small holding force led by Sandy, Gray's mother, in the old Razor Shiver section of the Riptide territory. Gray hoped the battle would not touch that area.

"Hear, hear!" added Silversun.

Whalem slowed from his sprint swim. "Their advance scouts are battling with ours!"

"What does their main force look like? Size? Formation?" asked Silversun, flicking his fins up and down.

"Not as many as we thought. We're even in numbers!"

"There's some good news!" said Grinder.

Whalem continued, "They're in a single horde of a thousand, moving in a diamond formation. We can't get close enough to see the absolute lineup, but it seems to be an even distribution of different sharkkind. And more good news, a bunch are undersized!"

"You can't eat properly if you're always fighting, I guess," Gray said, a little too quietly.

"Only one horde?" asked Quickeyes. "What luck! Maybe the others got some sense and deserted that crazy fish."

Lochlan swished his tail through the cold water, thinking. "Indi's armada is much bigger than that."

"Perhaps they've taken losses in a previous battle on their way here," reflected Silversun. "Maybe they couldn't replace their mariners fast enough?"

"Might be," Lochlan said. "But let's stay keen. There may be another force out there. I'll have Whalem send scouts to make sure they don't go for our tails during the battle."

"Good thinking," said Grinder.

"Let's form up!" Lochlan boomed. "Everyone in position and at the hover!" The golden great white turned to Gray as everyone else went off to their positions. "You understand I would do this, if I could."

"I know," Gray answered. He could smell Lochlan's blood leaking from the ghastly wound on his flank. Despite the best efforts of the doctor and surgeonfish, it had not closed.

"Don't be nervous. If you get confused, do what your gut tells you!"

"Is that a fat joke?" Gray said, smiling the best he could, which wasn't much. The quip fell flat to his ears.

Lochlan thought it was great, though. "That's the stuff, mate! You can do this!"

Gray got into the diamondhead position. Even though it sounded like the fin in the diamondhead should be the absolute first, that wasn't the case. Gray swam four rows back with the largest and fiercest Auzy-Auzy mariners arranged directly in front to protect him. It gave the shark in that position a perfect view of the battle waters.

"Advance, ahead slow," Gray said, his mouth so dry it came out a squeaky whisper. But Olph the dolph's sharp ears heard and clicked out the command. Everyone moved forward.

Gray struggled to control his breathing, not letting his gills pant too fast. That always made you look winded or nervous. He didn't want to give either impression.

I have to be strong, he thought.

Then Gray saw the Indi mariners.

"There they are!" cried someone many rows below as the Black Wave slid into view. Of Finnivus there was no sign. But Gray's heart leapt. It wasn't the huge, overwhelming force he expected. In fact, Riptide United's formation was almost as big! Gray's tension fell away. A few seconds after seeing the enemy, a totally unexpected feeling rose inside of Gray. They could do it. *He* could do it. They could win!

The Indi formation split itself into two triangles, small ends joining in the middle. Gray shifted his mariners accordingly. The Indi armada came forward, speeding up. They seemed a bit sloppier than usual. Not everyone was perfectly in position as he had seen them before.

Gray increased their speed. "Ten strokes!" he yelled. It looked as if the two formations were going to strike each other head on. Gray was glad. That way he wouldn't have to give any orders at all!

But something nagged at him. This was a much simpler attack than Indi was known for. Usually they split into several battle fins which feinted and nibbled, pulling an opposing force apart before striking a crushing blow. Maybe the Indi mariners were tired of fighting—so exhausted they weren't thinking clearly.

He got a closer look at the attackers. Something was wrong. Not every shark had the Black Wave tattoo, marking them as armada members. Then Gray realized.

They were all pups!

Every single one!

This wasn't the Indi armada at all! The evil Finnivus knew that sharkkind, especially the females, would hesitate sending a pup to the Sparkle Blue. And this was an armada of kids!

"Gray!" shouted Jaunt from her subcommander position. "Orders!"

"They're pups!" he shouted. "They're all pups!" Olph

the battle dolph made a razzing noise of disapproval above him.

"It doesn't matter! Orders!"

Gray's mind reeled. It was a key moment and he did . . .

Nothing.

But suddenly—Lochlan was there!

He was swimming so fast! The golden great white cut through the pup formation, bashing the guards away to give a tremendous tail slap to its leader, a large boy tiger shark.

"You can't catch me, you jelly-drifting flipper!" he shouted as he darted away from the Indi formation, creating a huge mess.

The youngling leader was enraged! He took off after Lochlan, shouting, "I'll kill you!"

"Protect the leader!" Lochlan shouted at the Indi formation. And while Gray could see that the golden great white was the one saying it, the Indi mariners couldn't! They tore off after their angry commander. Soon, all the pups were madly following—and more importantly—not attacking, Gray's formation!

But Lochlan couldn't get away. The wound in his side opened as if it were new, streaming a thick trail of black blood. The pups grew mad with the scent. They bumped and bit one another as they struggled to get at Lochlan.

Just as he was overtaken, the golden great white

made a furious turn and got above his pursuers. He smiled at the Riptide United mariners, waggling his fins. "To victory!" he cried out in a strong and clear voice. And just before the frenzied cluster of Indi pup mariners engulfed him, Lochlan *winked* at Gray. Then the AuzyAuzy King was swarmed by hundreds of sharks as the pups went into a feeding frenzy.

"Loch!" yelled Gray.

Suddenly, a second group of Indi mariners smashed into their formation. They were only five hundred, but these were *real* Black Wave mariners. They rammed the center of Gray's formation, right under the diamond-head, throwing his defenders out of position.

"We've got to withdraw!" shouted Mari, as she fought off an attack by a ferocious blue shark. Even though Riptide United vastly outnumbered these new attackers, the Black Wave mariners knew what they were doing.

And we're totally disorganized and drifting dead in the water, Gray thought, a cold dread gripping him.

But what to order? Swim Away? They would be caught from behind and slaughtered. Swordfish Parries? How could that be used? That was wrong to even get inside his head. Then Gray couldn't think of anything *but* Swordfish Parries! He forgot every other move! Gray was paralyzed by indecision!

Time slowed as sharkkind died all around him, spiraling away to the Sparkle Blue. Soon the Indi mariners would smash completely through their formation.

Suddenly there was a whirling ball of water growing in front of them. Gray's eyes adjusted as everything got brighter. "Hold steady at the hover!" he shouted. Olph repeated his order. Gray found the source between their massed formation and the bulk of the Indi battle fins—it was Takiza!

"YOU LUMPFISH SHALL NOT PASS!" the little betta's voice boomed, impossibly loud. The light grew brighter and brighter, and the Black Wave's formation melted as their mariners gave in to panic. They bumped and jostled one another to get away. This chaos rippled and cascaded across their tight formation, destroying it. The pups scattered also, retreating as fast as they were able. Their feeding frenzy was no match for the terror that Takiza was inspiring.

"Left turn, ahead slow," Gray said, and Olph relayed that to everyone. "Jaunt, you have the diamondhead. Take them in. Run patrols and have Onyx and Barkley swim out and keep an eye on where those enemy sharks are going!"

"But I want to—"

"I'll look for him!" Gray said. "You follow orders! Finnivus and the rest of Indi could be anywhere!"

"Yes sir!" Jaunt shot back, but she wasn't happy about it.

Gray went to the area where he last saw Lochlan. Takiza's turbulent power had cleared the area of blood, but not of dead pups. Of the golden great white, there was no sign.

"Lochlan!" Gray said in a clear voice. Since the warring parties had left, it was so quiet. The dwellers in the area had all been smart enough to swim away. "Loch, if you're hiding, now's the time to come out!"

"Nulo, stop," Takiza said in a firm voice, floating in front of his right eye.

"But I'm trying to find—"

Takiza slashed his fins through the water, cutting him off. "Lochlan boola Naka Fiji swims the Sparkle Blue now."

The cold current carried away Gray's tears.

Mari watched the two from a distance. Though she knew Takiza was there, her eyes were glued on Gray. Her friend had suffered another, almost unimaginable, loss. King Lochlan was like a big brother to Gray, though she doubted her friend fully realized this.

She gagged, the smell of blood drifting in the water interrupting her thoughts.

And it was the blood of pups!

Mari pictured her stomach as a stone to stop from heaving everything she had eaten for the last week into the water. Finnivus was evil! How could he order children to fight? Didn't they know their lives were being used as a distraction, to be thrown away so the real Black Wave mariners could complete their surprise attack? Of course they didn't, she thought, answering her own question.

But her larger concern was Gray, who she saw was crying freely. Would he be all right? He absolutely froze in the battle, but who wouldn't? Mari knew that Gray could be a great leader one day, but they didn't have many more days. King Lochlan was gone, and Gray had even more doubts about himself than before.

Just five hundred Black Wave mariners had almost destroyed them. And Finnivus and the real armada were swimming toward them to finish the task. Mari's stomach clenched again, and fear crept like an icy urchin down her spine.

Could Gray recover in time?

One way or another, they would get their answer soon.

CHAPTER 12

GRAY PAUSED, OUT ALONE IN FRONT OF THE massed mariners of the Riptide, AuzyAuzy, Hammer, and Vortex Shivers, as well as many of the refugees that had been streaming into their homewaters in hopes of safety. It was silent in the cool waters with the sun shining from the chop-chop above and colorful terraced greenie behind him. He wished Takiza was here to tell him what to say, but the unpredictable betta was gone once more.

In a loud voice Gray began, "King Lochlan boola Naka Fiji was a great leader and a good friend of mine." He picked his mother, Sandy, out of the crowd, and she nodded, her barbels vibrating with emotion. Even though she hadn't known Lochlan the way Gray had, she had a tender heart and was moved by his death, as was everyone.

"His sacrifice saved us from Finnivus and the Indi

armada. He taught me so much about being a leader, about being a good fin. I wish I were a better student. But as he swims the Sparkle Blue, I know he's watching over us. With all my heart, I want to tell you that the danger is over, but it's not. That was only their first attack. The Indi sharks were pushed away this time, but a larger force is coming. The Black Wave is swimming toward us. I'm asking you to stay and face the danger, face Finnivus's evil."

Gray saw the mariners were putting on a brave face even though they had doubts. He needed to rally them, but his heart was heavy. The loss of Lochlan was so huge. The golden great white was the bond that kept everyone together. How could Gray hope to take his place? He couldn't.

"We will continue to swim and be ready. We will not be caught by surprise. And when we meet Finnivus and his mariners for real . . . we will, umm, we will fight."

The gathered fins had expected more, and there was a low murmur. They picked up on Gray's doubts. That he was no leader. That Lochlan was wrong about him. Gray was about to admit this when Striiker bellowed, "You heard him! There's no time for lazy summer swims. Mariners of Riptide, we have work to do! AuzyAuzy, Hammer, and Vortex check with your commanders."

Thankfully Grinder and Silversun immediately ordered their mariners to combat drills as Jaunt did the same with AuzyAuzy. Striiker slapped Gray on the flank with his tail as he passed and said, "Good speech."

Followed by Jaunt, Mari came over, her lobed thresher tail switching back and forth in short, hesitant strokes. "Are you okay, Gray?"

"I'm fine," Gray told Mari; then asked Jaunt, "Is there any word?"

"We sent a messenger but no answer," Jaunt told him. "Indi has been taking out our scouts, though." The small tiger waggled her fins. "I'm thinking you're wrong, if you're looking for another opinion."

"I'm not."

"What's this about?" asked Mari.

Gray turned to his friend as Barkley and Whalem joined them. "I told Jaunt to send for Xander or Kendra to replace me."

Kendra and Xander del Hav'aii were first and third in the Line for AuzyAuzy, but more importantly they were royalty and could take command of the mariners. But both were busy fighting in the Sific against Indi's large and powerful holding. Could either leave where they were so badly needed? It would take time. Perhaps time Gray wouldn't have before the next attack. But he wanted a leader whom their fins would follow without question. "Everyone here deserves someone better than me."

"That's dumb!" Barkley exclaimed.

"Your friend is right," agreed Whalem.

Mari gasped. "Gray, no! We won the battle! Kind of..."

"There is no kind of! I'm not fit to command!" he said, a bit louder than he wanted. "I froze out there! If it weren't for Takiza, we would all be dead."

Gray watched as Barkley swished his tail, not making eye contact. At least Barkley knew it was true, though he wouldn't say it out loud. "Where's Takiza?" the dogfish asked instead. "If he promises to be there, everyone will be okay with you leading."

Gray shook his head at his friend. "Don't you think I asked? We can't count on him. Apparently he has more important things to do."

"Whatever the betta is doing is none of our concern," Whalem said. "You're our leader. Forget Takiza and concentrate on that."

"Grinder and Silversun don't have confidence in me. I can see it in their eyes. They'll leave if I stay in charge."

"Well, we're behind you one hundred percent," Mari told him.

"You shouldn't be!" Gray shot back. "Without Hammer and Vortex Shivers, we lose! It's that simple!" He looked over at the battle-scarred tiger shark. "Whalem—"

"No, son. I'm not up to the task," the tiger answered before he was asked. It was amazing Whalem could continue to do everything he was doing.

"Enough!" Barkley said. "There is no one else, so deal with it, Gray. This isn't an assignment in Miss Lamprey's class you can blow off. Quit feeling sorry for yourself and just do it!"

"I'm glad you have that opinion," Gray said. "Because I've decided to promote you to subcommander. You're about to be a much more important part of our plans. At least I can do that right."

Barkley let out a shocked, "Whaaat?!"

Gray felt his anger growing. He knew it was because of the soul-crushing pressure, but he didn't have time to coddle Barkley. Not today. "You say I should quit whining, well, right back at you! It's time for you to fin up!" Gray snapped.

Jaunt and Mari were surprised, both by the promotion and Gray's outburst. Whalem, though, gave Barkley a thoughtful look and nodded.

Barkley sputtered, his tail nervously twitching. "Please, I didn't mean—"

Gray cut his friend off. "Here's what you're going to do: Pick ten of the best mariners we have and train them to sneak around as well as you can. Our scouts are getting caught and killed out there. And they didn't even realize that Finnivus had sent pups against us in a sneak attack! They need to do better." Gray nodded at Whalem. "No offense to you."

"None taken," Whalem said. "We lost another patrol yesterday, and I do fear the worst. We're getting slaughtered out there. Any help Barkley can provide would be—"

"This is crazy!" Barkley exclaimed.

"You want me to lead? Well, here's me leading," Gray said in a more even tone.

"But—but—no one will listen to me!" Barkley whined. "I'm just a dogfish!"

"You've never thought of yourself as 'just a dogfish,' Barkley. Now I need you to prove it to others," Gray told him. "And it will help me, so do it.

"But—"

Gray cut Barkley off. "You have your orders!"

Barkley looked like he was about to burst into tears. The dogfish yelled as he swam away, "You're doing this out of spite, you fat lumpfish!"

Mari looked at Gray as if he were a type of shark she'd never seen before, which, in fact, he was.

"What?" he asked. "He can do it. I have confidence in him. Just like you all have confidence in me."

"But we actually *do* have confidence in you," Mari said.

"Ask yourself if that matters to Finnivus," Gray told them as he swam away from the training field. He could feel every eye follow him as he left. How could what was supposed to be a day to honor his friend Lochlan have gone so horribly wrong?

CHAPTER 13

VELENKA WATCHED THE FRENZY AS THE *squaline* tore through the Riptide scouts that had been captured in the last few days of their relentless swim to the North Atlantis. Though Velenka didn't mind the blood coloring the waters red, she was happy the armada had stopped. The pace that Finnivus ordered was grueling. The Black Wave would be within striking distance of Gray and his sharkkind within a week.

"Excellent!" cried Finnivus from his position above the floating royal court. "My *squaline* are invincible!"

Velenka was relieved that the emperor was in a good mood even after the defeat of his surprise attack, although he didn't call it a defeat. He had raged about Takiza spoiling his fun. But the report that King Lochlan boola Naka Fiji had been sent to the Sparkle Blue by the pup mariners raised the emperor's spirits immediately. He was so giddy he laughed his high-pitched, tittering cackle for a full hour as everyone watched in mute astonishment.

It was terrifying. The emperor was mad, completely mad.

Finnivus had made a mistake by only sending five hundred mariners in the secondary surprise attack force. The rest were made to guard his royal turtleness in case of a *reverse* sneak attack. As if Lochlan or Gray would be stupid enough to meet the Indi armada on unfamiliar currents and in the open waters. If the emperor had sent another five hundred of the Black Wave, the war would be over.

Whether I live or die will *not* be decided in the chaos of a battle, Velenka thought.

Finnivus ate one of the mangled prisoners immediately, not waiting for the royal seasoners to do their work. He stopped in mid-bite and looked over at the sharkkind of the royal court. "Am I to eat alone? Join in! This feast will whet your appetites for when we dine on the mariners of the Golden Rush and their new leader, *Gray*." The emperor knew that Gray was the one commanding the revitalized Riptide Shiver from the leaders of his surprise attack force, which had rejoined the main armada.

The royal court ate. Velenka swam over and pretended to eat also. "It's good, isn't it?" he asked her.

"Delicious!" she answered while shaking a carcass from side to side. She made sure not to swallow any, though.

That would be bad.

Finnivus became thoughtful and pouty. "My plan would have worked! That frilly little dweller spoiled everything! But he can't do it every time! No, he can't! We will attack again, and soon, before he can recover!"

Apparently Finnivus had met Takiza a few times when he was growing up. Indi Shiver had even done a study on the Siamese fighting fish in case they had to fight him one day. Long ago Takiza had power to do almost anything he wanted. But that was no longer the case; the little dweller was getting weaker as he aged. There were reports that when Takiza performed a large magic, such as he did when he led the AuzyAuzy mariners from the Sific to the battle that must not be named, he had to rest for many days afterward.

"They will feel my wrath!" Finnivus said, fever brightness in his eyes. He coughed, and Velenka stopped herself from smiling, lest the emperor see it. "The entire Atlantis will be taught a lesson by me and my Armada of Justice. I will, umm, *we* will dispense royal justice by sending every sharkkind swimming against me to the Sparkle Blue for disobeying our will!" He laughed again, the high giggle grating up and down Velenka's spine.

"Your plan was a wonder, Emperor," she said, smacking her teeth as if she had enjoyed a piece of one of the prisoners.

"Of course! I thought it up!" he said smugly, tapping his tail on the blue whale that was currently underneath him.

Finnivus leaned against the Speakers Rock embedded in the whale's back. She had asked Tydal the know-it-all court shark how that was done. It seemed that when the blue whales were pups, the area in their backs was eaten away to snugly hold the symbol of Indi Shiver power. The mobile throne was a potent tribute to Indi Shiver's might and ruthlessness for everyone in the Big Blue to see. It showed that they owned the waters wherever they swam.

Velenka longed to rest herself on the backs of those whales. She wanted all the fools in the royal court to drive their snouts into the muck whenever *she* commanded! In time they would. Velenka swore this to herself. She would be empress of the seas!

Finnivus went on: "We knew the Golden Rush would be too sensitive to defend themselves against my pup soldiers! It makes them weak, not being able to do everything that's necessary to be the greatest emperor there has ever been!"

The emperor turned to the rows of pup mariners, allowed publicly in the court for the first time. They were trying their best to maintain an attention hover as Finnivus shouted, "Isn't that right, my children?"

The group raggedly dipped their snouts and shouted, "MY LIFE FOR YOU!"

Finnivus preened to the court. "They love me, even more than you do. Perhaps, one day, they will replace you all." He cackled as those in the court fidgeted in nervous silence, twitching fins and swishing tails. "I—*we*—are only kidding. But as you can see, my pup mariner force certainly did not *opud*!" The emperor tittered, and this time everyone joined in.

The pups were under strict guard, of course. The emperor's plan had been hatched in the weeks after the battle that could not be named. It was this idea that got Finnivus out of his funk after they fled from Riptide to the Indi homewaters. Of course, pups were always taken and trained to be part of Indi's armada when another shiver was defeated. This was nothing new. But after he got his idea, Finnivus began destroying shivers *just* to take their *pups*! This was a new and, Velenka thought, admirable, twist. The emperor gathered the young from all over the Big Blue and had them taught to worship him as if he were the second coming of Tyro.

He couldn't use Indi Shiver pups for this, of course. That would cause a riot from their parents and the other royals in the court. And these pups weren't even the sons and daughters of those in the armada. Again, that would probably have gotten Finnivus a bite to the gills. But the pups from the shivers he conquered—they were fair game.

Their parents were sent to the Sparkle Blue and used to feed the armada. Then Finnivus had the younglings taught that he was their protector. He gave them the best of everything. He made them know they were important and vital to the defense of the Indi homewaters and also that the forces against them were the ones who killed their parents.

Finnivus said everything a young and impressionable pup would want to hear. And soon, they were willing to lay down their lives at the emperor's command. The pups were too young to be actual mariners in anything but name only—and would be ground into paste by a well-trained force—but that wasn't the point.

Though Velenka herself would not care what age an enemy was—she would kill without hesitation—sharkkind with children *did* care. In the training battles against other shivers, Velenka saw that the other forces hated fighting the young pups, some of them barely old enough to speak. Especially those who were parents. And who would know to sort a battle fin by parenthood? No one! Their formations became useless! That was when the superbly trained Indi armada would sweep in and destroy them. It was a brilliant and merciless plan.

Velenka decided she could not afford to be any less ruthless and began swimming her own current to be empress of the Big Blue. She watched in satisfaction as Finnivus coughed and paled slightly.

"Take the rest of this away, Tydal!" Finnivus yelled

at the brown and yellow epaulette shark. "The Riptide flippers I'm—*we*—are eating—they do not agree with me!"

"Yes, Your Magnificence!" Tydal said, nosing what was left of the carcass into the court area. Others hovering there finished it with gusto. They loved to feast on the emperor's scraps. Velenka smiled on the inside as she noted a few more sickened faces in the royal court.

Eat up, she thought. Have your fill.

What Finnivus and the court didn't know was that they were being poisoned.

Velenka had learned many things in her studies when she was younger. One list she memorized well was the different types of poison greenie. It was rare, this greenie. Velenka went off searching in every area where they stopped for food and finally found a good amount of one particularly toxic variety called revulent. It had been easy to hide in the royal baggage area where Finnivus kept a few comforts from the Indi homewaters such as coral representations of his likeness that he enjoyed looking at and the blooms of sea flowers that he thought were fragrant. Only a little bit of revulent fed to the prisoners poisoned their flesh for a week afterward. Sometimes the prisoners could barely swim! And Finnivus wondered why they defended themselves so poorly.

Velenka only needed them to stay alive long enough to feed the emperor.

"My Magnificence," Velenka said. "Are you sure you

won't eat some more? You must keep up your strength if you are to defeat those cowards!"

Finnivus nodded. "You're right. Bring me some of what you're having." Velenka dutifully swam over with a large flank in her mouth and placed it before the emperor. He took a tentative bite and grunted in approval. "Yes, this is better."

With a flick of his royal tail, Finnivus dismissed her and spoke to everyone present. "We didn't really want our first plan to succeed," said Finnivus between bites. "It wouldn't be any fun! No, I must be watching when we crush those traitors! We will be victorious, or my name isn't Finnivus Victor! Tail stroke by tail stroke we swim ever closer to our destiny!"

Velenka and everyone else cheered loudly.

And every bite the emperor took brought him a tail stroke closer to the Sparkle Blue.

And a tail stroke closer to my own shining future, Velenka thought.

CHAPTER 14

"AGAIN!" TAKIZA YELLED IN THE DARKNESS AND cold at the training fields near the Maw.

Gray sighed and forced himself to go on. He was exhausted, mentally and physically, almost at the breaking point. And still Takiza pressed him. The betta had returned from wherever he had mysteriously gone, without telling Gray anything about it. There was plenty of time for insults, though.

"You are a megalodon, yet you display the strength of an injured anemone!"

Gray struggled in the snug embrace of the greenie harness. This one was the biggest that Takiza had ever woven for him. And it contained a boulder! Not a rock, an actual boulder!

Gray whipped his tail back and forth as he strained to swim through the obstacle course of urchin-spine-sharp coral spires. "Faster, faster!" the betta urged. Gray grunted and huffed, his gills pumping furiously. Takiza swam serenely in front of his left eye. "Miraculous. For once, you haven't the strength to complain. Perhaps we should always train at this level."

The new course was so long that Gray despaired and let the boulder hit the seabed with a *thump*. "I can't do it," he gasped. "I just can't."

"You can't? Or is it that you *won't*?"

"I can't! Can-not!" Gray yelled. "I would if I could, but I can't! And let me guess, here's the part where you tell me how Lochlan was able to lift a rock three times this size and swim through the course while singing the AuzyAuzy fight song. But *I* can't!" Gray felt his body go slack. He had nothing left. "This is pointless. Why are you making me do this?" he whispered to himself.

"We are doing this because you are good for nothing else *but* lifting heavy rocks."

Gray chuckled. "I don't think this is the time for jokes." He looked up just in time to get a stinging slap to his snout. "Ow! What was that for?"

"It wasn't a joke. It was an insult, yet you are too dim to understand it as such," the betta said, dead serious. "You are useless in the battle against Finnivus. Better you spend time here, moving rocks, and let the others fight without you."

Gray glared and tried to leave before saying something bad to Takiza, but the harness yanked him back.

"Okay, I'm done! Get me out of here. I need to get back to the homewaters."

"For what? Because you are bored? I am not bored. Lift."

"I *don't* want to do this anymore!" Gray shouted. He felt tears coming to his eyes and shook his head side to side as hard as he could to stop them. He felt embarrassed and shamed for some reason.

Takiza slashed his gauzy fins through the water. "You do not want to do many things, Nulo. The list grows longer with each day, even as Finnivus draws nearer."

Gray strained against the greenie harness. It held him tight. "Which is why we shouldn't be here! I should be—I should be . . . should be . . ."

"Should be—?" asked the betta crossly. "Training to lead a massed formation to victory?"

"For one thing!" Gray shouted. "Yes! Take this harness off, Takiza! Now!"

"I do not believe I will. I think it would be better for your friends to have no leader at all, than be led by you." Takiza gave him another stinging slap on his snout. It was loud even in the heavy waters of the training field and made a cracking noise that echoed among the coral spires. "I say this because you would fail, wouldn't you, Nulo? You-would-*fail*! Say it!"

Gray gasped in physical pain from the words. It felt as if Takiza had released a magic that entered his body and exploded his heart into pieces.

Tears began gushing from Gray's eyes. "You want me to say it? That's all I think about day and night! It kills me that I can't be the leader they need!" he said, fins trembling in utter dejection.

"Then we are agreed," Takiza said softly in Gray's ear. "You would fail, so there's no reason for you to do anything but move a large stone because I tell you to do it."

Gray felt his anger rising. "Shiro, stop..."

Takiza was eerily calm, drifting in front of Gray. "I will say what I want, and there's nothing you can do to change that."

"Shut up!" Gray shouted. "Shut up, now!"

"You cannot stop me, Nulo. I do what I please, just as Finnivus will do as he pleases ... with everyone you love."

"DON'T SAY THAT!" Gray screeched.

"What will you do? *Nothing*?" Takiza asked in a mocking voice that seemed to scratch Gray's mind.

"I don't deserve this! I don't! Leave me alone!"

But the betta continued hovering in front of Gray, his eyes boring into him. "Your friends will swim the Sparkle Blue because you can do *nothing* to prevent it. Your mother will swim the Sparkle Blue because you utterly *failed*. And your brother and sister will also swim the Sparkle Blue, again, because you were good for ... *nothing*."

"NO-NO-NO! Gray struggled against the harness, trying to swim away from Takiza. He didn't want to hear this! He tried to flee from the betta's cutting words, but the greenie harness held him tight.

"You have managed to lose the battle before you swam a single stroke. You will fail *everyone* you know and love—without even giving a token effort to save their lives from the horror that is Finnivus. He will do what he pleases with them . . . as I do with you right now."

Gray shot straight at Takiza. If it weren't for the boulder in the harness, he would have chomped down on the betta. As it was, his teeth came together in a thundering crash inches away from Takiza as he calmly hovered in the cold water.

The Siamese fighting fish shook his head in disappointment. "It's a wonder you can feed yourself, Nulo. You are pathetic." The little betta turned and slowly swam away.

"Come back here right now! This isn't over!" Gray's tears were gone, and he felt hot anger rising. Takiza was wrong to be so cruel, and he would admit that. One way or another, he was going to! "Don't you show your tail to me!" Gray shouted.

"If you wish another view, I suggest you do something about it," the betta said in a voice that made Gray grind his teeth. But he was still tied tight to an immovable boulder!

Gray tried shooting forward to snap the tether but was jerked to a halt. Takiza knew what he was doing when he wove it, and the greenie refused to break.

Then I'll just have to lift it.

With colossal effort, Gray churned his tail as fast as he could. So much of the seabed flew up from his powerful tail strokes that Gray felt as if he were in a storm of silt and grit. But slowly, the boulder did rise. And out of that sandy cloud swam Gray. He chased after Takiza, swaying left and right as the fast current got a hold of the giant boulder hanging beneath him. "You're not getting away that easy! You're going to hear what I have to say, *Shiro!*"

Suddenly Takiza was again in front of his left eye, swishing his frilly fins in annoyance. "What is it you think you deserve, Nulo? Oh, do enlighten me. Tell me your thoughts so that I may bask in their genius."

"First of all, you're very sarcastic! It's annoying!" Gray gasped, the weight of the massive boulder crushing him through the harness. "It's not a fitting way for you to speak, and especially *teach*, you being so old and *supposedly* wise." The strong, icy current wasn't helping matters. And maddeningly, Takiza declined to swim in a straight line, making it even harder to keep up!

"So," Takiza mused. "You understand that I am wise? Perhaps our training was not a total waste."

"That's—that's—" Gray grunted as he followed the betta around a coral pylon. "That's not the point I was making, you preening little puffer fish!" Takiza gave Gray a wounded look but let him continue. "This isn't fair!"

"And who told you life in the open waters was *fair?*" Takiza asked. "Please let me know who that wise fin was so I may go for their learned guidance in matters both large and small."

"There's that sarcastic edge again," Gray grunted, using the current to his advantage and clearing an obstacle that Takiza had swum around. "It makes you sound like a cranky shellhead. Is that what you're going for? Because that's what I'm getting."

I'll show him, Gray thought. I'm going to win this argument if I have to carry this boulder through the seven seas!

"And we do things because they're *fair* all the time! If I have two fish and my friend has none, I would give my friend a fish—probably the smaller one—but hey, I'm pretty big."

"Some would say too big," Takiza added.

"That's not the point!"

"Oh, please let there be a point aside from the one on your sizeable snout."

"The *point* is, I shouldn't be expected to do everything!" Gray yelled. "You know who should lead? *You* should lead!"

"I cannot."

"Can-not or *will* not?" said Gray, imitating Takiza as best he could.

The betta nodded. "There are limits to my powers. And I fear a greater threat than Finnivus now swims the oceans. So someone else must lead *this* battle while I counter that threat." Takiza ruffled his fins as if the conversation were over.

The heck it was! Gray churned after the betta, catching up once more.

"Everyone looks to me like I'm the fin with all the answers. Why would they do that?"

"Perhaps it is because you are a megalodon and should not exist."

"They don't know that, and I didn't ask to be a megalodon!" Gray shouted, his voice squeaking more than he would have liked from his straining effort. "I have no idea why Lochlan picked me to lead his mariners. Come on, they're a *royal* shiver! Why would he choose me?"

"Because he knew you could stop Finnivus, just as I knew you could lift the boulder and carry that burden successfully, a burden that Lochlan himself never even got off the ground," Takiza said matter-of-factly.

"It's impossible. I can't do it!" Gray yelled in reply.

Takiza motioned with his tail at the obstacle course. "But you already have." The betta gave the harness a tail flick, and the whole thing fell off. Gray looked back and was dumbstruck at the distance he had moved the huge rock. It *was* impossible.

But somehow, he had done it.

"How . . . ?" Gray asked in a whisper.

"How indeed, my young apprentice?" Takiza swam in front of Gray's eye, looking him over, as if deciding something. In short order, the betta nodded and said, "Yes, I do believe it's time."

"Time for what?"

"Time for your favorite thing, Nulo. Answers. Lochlan gave leadership to you, rather than those with more experience and standing, because he thought you were the only one who could do the impossible. To defeat the unbeatable! He thought you were the embodiment of a legend."

"I understand the words you said, but not the way you said them."

Takiza sighed, irritated. "It's always two strokes forward, then one back with you, isn't it?"

"I don't understand that either. I'm really, *really* tired."

Takiza made an exaggerated groan. "This is why my advice for you to keep quiet is so very wise in your particular case, Nulo. Listen, as I attempt to enlighten you. I shall now recite an ancient prophecy, known by only a chosen few, Lochlan and myself among them.

> *"He shall come from the depths*
> *of oceans prehistore.*
> *He will face an evil empire*
> *as from the ancient lore.*
> *Raised in warm Caribbi waters,*
> *by coral adored,*
> *by coral abhorred,*
> *a megalodon will arise*
> *and win the unwinnable war."*

Gray looked at Takiza and repeated the verse to himself.

The line *"raised in warm Caribbi waters, by coral adored, by coral abhorred"* was freakishly specific to him, as he was from Coral Shiver, loved by his mother but also banished at one time. Gray's tail twitched as he asked, "And you—*you*—think *that* is about me? *You* think that?"

"One never knows about legends," Takiza answered. "They are irritatingly unclear. But the verse does seem to be speaking of someone remarkably like you, in an uncomfortably similar situation to the one we find ourselves in today."

"And Lochlan believed this? Believed in me?" Gray asked.

"He did," Takiza answered. Then after a moment, he added, "As do I."

"Wow."

Takiza began swimming off. "I am done teaching for the day, Nulo. But there is no reason you cannot continue to learn as you make your way home."

CHAPTER 15

BARKLEY WATCHED AS THE TWO SHARKS FROM Hammer Shiver, Sledge and Peen, went through the greenie in the Hydenseek, a dense kelp field off the Riptide homewaters. They were making the same mistakes he did when discovering what worked and what didn't to swim with stealth. When Gray hurled this promotion at him—forcing him to create a new kind of sneakier scout—Barkley was sure Gray was doing it because he was mad at his own situation.

Just the same, Barkley soon found out that leading was *waaaay* harder than he had ever imagined. He didn't know how Gray held up at all under the strain of being the big fin for the entire armada. Barkley was older by a month—a fact he loved to remind Gray about whenever he got the chance—but even if he liked to consider himself more mature, he was finding it impossible to lead just *ten* sharkkind, much less every single shark living in the Riptide homewaters.

"Too fast!" Barkley yelled after slipping directly over their dorsal fins. Both sharks were surprised by his sudden appearance and twitched as if they'd been shocked by an eel. "When you're swimming against the current, you have to let the greenie *slide* past you, or a sharp-eyed guard will notice it's not moving the right way."

The hammerheads weren't thankful for this information, or even embarrassed for being totally startled. Just the opposite. They were angry.

"Oh, yeah? Then we'd fight whoever found us!" said Peen, the smaller, more aggravating hammerhead. The second, Sledge, was much larger. He added, "This sneaking around isn't for us. It's for jellies and turtles!"

Barkley seethed. The hammerheads were mariners, and while they wouldn't physically harm him—Grinder gave them strict orders to obey—they didn't take him seriously at all.

Stupid Gray! Barkley thought. Why is he making me do this, anyway? To show what a giant failure I am at everything?

"Fins up!" Barkley yelled as gruffly as he could. He thought that the stern tone would make him sound tougher. Upon hearing his new voice the first time, though, Mari had asked if he had a cold. But at least Mari *wanted* to learn.

And then there was Snork . . .

"Yes, sir!" the sawfish shouted. "Right away, sir!"

While Barkley appreciated the sawfish volunteering,

his enthusiasm wasn't helpful. In fact, it made the other tough mariners respect him even less. Everyone except Mari chuckled.

"You're all acting like you don't want to be here," Barkley began.

There was a snicker from inside the small company. Someone in the back coughed, "We don't!"

Oh, boy.

It had taken a few days of watching the mariners drill to make his choices. Barkley had seen something in each of these sharks that said they could be taught how to swim silently and unseen. When he got down to actually choosing, Barkley found that sharkkind, even of the same type, swam in very different ways. There was a small sub-set, usually those sharks who were smaller or slower when they were pups, which swam more efficiently and smoothly than the others. Normally, being small or slow would be a huge disadvantage, and those sharks mostly wouldn't make it to adulthood. The Big Blue was tough that way. You could either have lunch or *be* lunch on any given day. But the sharkkind that *did* overcome those deficits knew how it was to be weaker than those around them—and *still* survive.

Once these formerly weaker sharkkind grew into their bodies, they had learned something extra in the time the odds were against them. That also meant they were very hard to control.

Especially by me, Barkley thought. He took a deep

breath. "Well, I'll let you in on a secret—*I* don't want to be here, either! But we're under orders, and they come straight from the top. So let's make the best of it."

Mari watched him from the ranks. In her eyes Barkley could see that his speech needed something else. But what? "Your lives depend on what I'm teaching here, and how well you learn it!" Snork was smiling and waving his bill in agreement. Barkley saw he wasn't getting through to anyone else, though. "So get your snouts in that greenie and do it again!" The gathered sharks swam into the field, joking and tail slapping each other, not taking it seriously.

They don't take *me* seriously, he realized once again.

Barkley saw Grinder shake his head in disgust and swim away from Silversun, who hovered outside the training area, watching. Barkley had chosen three of Silversun's Vortex mariners to be in his special force, along with the two from Hammer Shiver. The rest were Riptide fins he already knew. But aside from Mari and Snork, they didn't hold a high opinion of Barkley either. The Vortex Shiver sharkkind, though—a mako, a blue, and a bull shark—were the most receptive.

Of course they are, Barkley thought. They're led by a small port jackson shark. They don't judge me by my size because they don't judge their leader by *his* size.

How did Silversun manage that trick?

"Mari, swim topside and yell out when you spot anyone! Last one found gets to leave early!" This did get a whooping, enthusiastic reaction from the recruits. Mari waggled her long lobed thresher tail at him and nodded.

Barkley swam over to Silversun. The Vortex leader waggled his pectoral fins in a greeting. "Interesting lessons, subcommander."

Barkley returned the greeting. "Yes, as you can see, I'm new at this. I need to get through to them, so, umm, this is kind of awkward, but can I ask—"

"I had to fight the biggest one," Silversun said.

"What?"

"You swam over to find out how I came to lead my shiver," the port jackson said. "It's a good question for you to ask at this time. It shows understanding of your specific problem, and a keen mind to know where the answer might hover."

"So, you're really smart, then." Barkley swished his tail back and forth.

"That remains to be seen," Silversun told him with a smile. "Hopefully, smart enough to not end up with my head on Finnivus's feeding platter."

"Okay, back to what I wanted to ask. So you beat someone up?"

"Yes, I did," Silversun said. "I'm not proud of it, but it had to be done. That shark is now first in my Line."

"The huge hammerhead?" Silversun's first was the biggest hammerhead anyone had ever seen! "That giant? You won a fight against *him*? Are you a Takiza-like, magical battler?" Barkley asked.

"Oh, no," Silversun laughed, shaking his blocky head. "I'm *terrible* at fighting!"

"But, then—how?"

Silversun glided closer to Barkley. "He would have ripped me apart in any fair fight, but I knew I needed to lead the shiver. I *knew* I would be better at it than him. You see, being the leader was the only way to protect my family, friends, and everyone else in the shiver."

"You cheated!"

Silversun waggled his tail sideways, meaning *not quite, but kind of.* "When the day came, I made sure that everything that could be in my favor *was* in my favor." Barkley thought that over, and Silversun added, "If you want them to listen, you need to prove to them you're worth listening to.

Barkley nodded thoughtfully. "Thanks, Silversun."

Mari called out another shark that she saw in the greenie. Over half were spotted in the short time Barkley was gone. In the real world, that would mean they were now dead.

They just have to be better, Barkley decided, as he swam over to them.

"Okay, everyone form up!" he yelled, forgetting about using his gruff voice and saying it normally. "I have a new drill that I think you'll enjoy. It's called, 'Beat up Barkley if you can!'"

Someone in the back said in a loud voice, "Now there's a drill we can get behind!" and everyone laughed.

Mari's eyes popped open. "Are you sure—"

"Yep! Today's your lucky day!" Barkley exclaimed. All the tension in his spine disappeared with an almost audible *whoosh*. "And before we start, go ahead, tell me what you really feel about what I'm trying to teach you." Barkley stopped right by the larger hammerhead, Sledge.

He became wary, as if Barkley were trying to trick him. He stiffened into attention hover with his eyes straight ahead and yelled, "Subcommander! I don't know what you mean, sir!"

Barkley slid around the two Hammer Shiver sharks. "I'm not that kind of a flipper, to get you in trouble with Grinder. You have my absolute permission to tell me *exactly* what you think of my lessons. That is, if you're brave enough to do that to my face." Barkley swished his tail in a way that Gray told him was *really* annoying. "Well, are you?"

"You . . . want the truth?" asked Sledge.

"I do!" yelled Barkley in his face. "So out with it!"

"I hate this assignment!" the large hammerhead said, getting louder as he went on. "I was gonna be right in the thick of things when we faced Indi armada! I coulda been the one that sent that chowderhead to the Sparkle Blue! But instead, here I am, nosing around in the greenie like some kind of krill-faced muck-sucker!"

There was dead silence from everyone. Sledge looked embarrassed, afraid he'd gone too far.

But Barkley took it in stride. He swam before his

small company, feeling better than at any time since he was promoted. "Do the rest of you feel the same way?"

There was a weak, mumbled agreement. "Come on, you puffers! I asked: Do the rest of you feel the same way? Yes or no?"

This time there was a tidal wave of loud agreement. Barkley nodded, swimming in front of them. "I'm gonna let you rejoin your units. *If* you can beat me in the greenie. Any and every one of you that successfully tags me with a move that would send me to the Sparkle Blue gets out of this assignment—with my permission."

There was excitement from the crew for the first time. There was even some respect in their eyes.

"But—and there's always a but—whoever *I* tag stays with me until Tyro comes and says you're done, with no more complaining. Do we have a deal?"

The sharks all snapped their tails and dipped their snouts, yelling, "Yes, sir!"

"Good!" Barkley told them as he swam toward the thick kelp bed. "Wait for two minutes, and then come after me. I will meet you in the greenie!"

It took only a minute for Barkley to totally disappear in the thick kelp of the Hydenseek. He felt serene as his unit came after him. He watched most everyone pass in their too fast and too wild search for him. A pair of Vortex Shiver sharks who had decided to work together swam within a tail length of him.

The third Vortex shark, and last of the recruits to come in the greenie, Barkley struck from below.

And so it went.

Barkley caught Peen as he came around a rock without checking first.

Sledge got a bump to the gills when he was lured into a thin gap by a brain coral formation.

The pair of Vortex sharks Barkley dealt with at the same time, both tail strikes.

He led two other recruits into the thickest greenie and thumped them in the flanks when they got turned around.

Snork he found lying in wait. The sawfish had picked an excellent spot but was given away when his gills puffed up too much sand.

And Mari—she was the toughest. She was already well-trained from the time they had spent together. But Mari was so busy looking for threats from below that she forgot to check topside. Big mistake.

Within two hours it was all over.

Barkley had stalked and ambushed each and every shark in his group. He earned their respect—and a nickname: Ghostfin.

After that, everyone listened. They kind of had to, after all ten of them were soundly beaten by a dog-fish. Ha! And Barkley discovered he *had* picked the correct sharkkind all right. They were gifted, lightning quick learners. And since they were some of the finest mariners in the armada *before* his training, in no time they could unleash complete destruction with the element of surprise that they now *always* had in their favor.

Soon, Barkley's "students" could run ambushes against three and four times their own number of regular mariners. In a one-on-one battle inside the greenie, they were simply unbeatable. The other mariners in the Riptide United forces began referring to their special corps as *Barkley's Ghostfins*, and the name stuck.

And when Finnivus finally arrived—now less than a week away—Barkley was determined that he and his ghostfins would help defeat the Black Wave armada.

CHAPTER 16

"WHY DOES MY STOMACH HURT SO MUCH?" whined Finnivus. He lolled sideways against the Speakers Rock atop the blue whale that carried him. The royal court rode behind the Indi armada, which led the way, its many mariners seeming to combine into a mega-predator. Drafting in the armada's wake, the royal court had an easy time of it and didn't even slow down for eating. The current was leading them inexorably to Velenka's old home at Riptide. She couldn't wait to see the death and destruction that the armada would inflict on Gray and his friends.

But *I* want to be the one who gives the order, she thought.

Finnivus groaned again. "Oh, I—*we*—hate this!"

"Perhaps you'd like a little something to settle your stomach, My Magnificence?" Velenka asked. Finnivus got himself to a more regal posture. He always liked it when she called him *My Magnificence.*

Finnivus smiled, clicking his perfectly aligned, notched teeth dramatically. "Perhaps we should keep our strength up! Tydal!"

"Yes, Emperor!" Quicker than a sea snake, Tydal the First Court Shark was there. "What is your wish?" The finja had nothing on Tydal in terms of sneaking around invisibly. And he was stuck with an epaulette shark's bright yellow and brown pattern all over his body! These were in addition to the two prominent black dots, one on each flank, which should have made him even more noticeable. But somehow, Tydal did abide.

"Have the royal seasoners prepare something." Finnivus gave it some thought and then added, "Sunfish, I think. Yes, sunfish. Let's make it hot and sweet, just like me." Finnivus led the court in a group laugh, until it ended with a deep, rattling cough.

Velenka smiled to herself. The emperor looked so pale and frail. His skin had turned a grayish color, quite unlike its former robust sheen. She had recently fed the prisoners a large amount of the poisonous revulent greenie. Just one more good dose should be enough to carry Finnivus to the Sparkle Blue.

"Why not a prisoner, Emperor Finnivus?" she asked.

Finnivus turned. "What?"

"Shouldn't we eat a prisoner to whet your appetite

for when you'll devour Gray?" Velenka put an adoring fervor into her eyes when she asked this.

Finnivus considered and called out to his court. "See why I, umm, *we*, plucked this mako from the muck and transformed her into a member of my royal court!"

Velenka felt herself actually preening. Apparently, she had grown fond of receiving attention from this fool! The sooner he was dead, the better.

Tydal zipped off but returned in a matter of moments.

"Your Majesty! The prisoners are all dead!"

Finnivus was in a good mood, though. Instead of flying into a rage at the epaulette, he smirked. "That's impossible! *We* did not order them that way!"

Tydal bobbed his head to the sandy seabed they were moving over. This was hard to do and maintain your distance from the royal blue whale, but the epaulette didn't put a fin out of place. "Forgiveness, Emperor Finnivus, I misspoke."

"Well, speak without doing that! You are beginning to *opud*."

Velenka sighed. The emperor was still trying to make everyone use the stupid word he made up.

Tydal dipped his head again. "What I meant to say is that all of our prisoners have died, without being killed by your order, or any of our sharkkind doing it. In fact, there are no bite marks." And then Tydal looked straight at Velenka. "It's as if they were . . . poisoned."

Velenka grew very still.

He *knows*.

The emperor roused himself, realization lighting up his eyes. His rage grew. "Tydal, are you saying the reason I am ill is because I—*we*—are poisoned?"

"I believe so, Your Majesty."

"STOP! STOP EVERYTHING!" Finnivus bellowed. The floating court slowed and then halted, sinking to the uneven ocean floor. The armada mariners didn't know what was going on, but the new mariner prime was no fool. He split his forces into battle fins and circled the court in a defensive screen.

Velenka asked accusingly, "How would you know the prisoners were poisoned, Tydal? Are you an expert in poisons?"

She hoped the epaulette would melt before her accusation, but he did not. Tydal answered calmly, "As First Court Shark, of course I am," he told everyone. "It's one of my duties. I test all the food from the royal seasoners. But I do not check the prisoners."

Oh, this was a disaster!

In Velenka's eagerness to poison Finnivus and the court, she had obviously given the prisoners too much revulent. Instead of tainting their flesh as she had planned, it killed them instead!

I can't believe my bad luck! she thought.

The emperor's eyes narrowed on Velenka, and she knew it was her life on the line now.

"You mean that someone who is an expert in poisons

could have been contaminating the prisoners' flesh to kill the emperor as he ate them?" Velenka asked.

"I cannot say for sure."

"You cannot, Tydal? Or you *will not* because it was *you* that betrayed our beloved emperor!"

Finnivus's eyes turned toward Tydal, who seemed calm as a windless lagoon in the summer. The emperor waited for the answer.

"I cannot say for sure because it's not for a lowly court shark to accuse anyone of anything."

"He seems guilty to me, Majesty!" Velenka interrupted.

But Tydal continued, "Which is why—just in case of something like this—I asked the captain of His Majesty's *squaline* to watch the prisoners as we traveled toward what will no doubt be a rousing victory over Riptide Shiver."

Velenka's insides froze.

Commander Hooktail, the new leader of the *squaline* swam forward from his position. He was a fat blue shark, one of the largest Velenka had ever seen. His body seemed to burst from its metallic armor covering.

Finnivus gestured with his tail. "Did you see anything odd, Hooktail? Speak! I command it!"

The muscled mariner bobbed his head. "Majesty, there were only three sharkkind from the royal court that went near the prisoner's cages, or the food served to them: Ashara, Klarion, and Velenka."

Velenka sprang into the silence before anyone else could. She knew that Ashara and Klarion were brother and sister and also members of the royal Line. It would have to be enough. "Emperor Finnivus! Ashara and Klarion must be trying to topple you! They are royalty! They want to lay themselves on your throne! I would never do anything like that!"

Klarion was struck dumb, but Ashara, his sister, shrieked, "You dare accuse me! You are the one! I had reason to be there!"

"Of course you did, you were poisoning my beloved emperor!" Velenka shot back, even though she knew this was a lie. Actually, the Indi mariner who had coughed during Finnivus's speech and was put in with the prisoners had been a family friend of theirs, and that was why they had visited.

But too bad! This was life and death.

"Lies!" shouted Klarion, who found his voice. "How could you think this, Majesty? We have both known you since we were pups!"

This seemed to have some effect on Finnivus, who nodded thoughtfully. Ashara then added, "And how well do any of us truly know Velenka? She would have said anything to survive when you conquered her puny shiver!"

"I offered my life to His Magnificence on that day!" Velenka answered calmly. Luckily, she had learned the history of Indi Shiver, knowing one day her life might depend on it. That day was today and the time was now. "My loyalty to Finnivus Victor Triumphant is as deep and as constant as the tides! But your family has always wanted to lie on Indi's coral throne! Treachery runs in your blood! Wasn't your grandfather executed for plotting against Finnivus's mighty father, Romulus? And here you are, doing the same thing while accusing me!"

Ashara and Klarion were aghast at having this family disgrace thrown in their faces and for a moment could say nothing. That was unfortunate for them. There was just enough truth in what Velenka said that Finnivus saw something in their eyes, or at least thought he did. Either way, it was a death sentence. He shouted, "Execute them!"

Ashara tried to make an excuse, and Klarion fought well. But both were dealt with in the end by the vicious *squaline*.

Then Finnivus looked Velenka's way. Again, her insides went cold. "And what are *we* supposed to do with you?"

"Emperor Finnivus, I would never do anything to harm you!" she cried. "I have loved you from the moment you spared my life! I wish only to serve you!" Finnivus swished his tail back and forth. Velenka made sure she looked sad and thoughtful and then struck with her most effective tactic.

Crying.

Between sobs she said, "If you do not believe me,

My Magnificence, then execute me this very moment and dine on my seasoned head! I only hope the meal is enjoyable for you as, you see, our family always did have bony heads. But with Tyro as my witness, I *will* swim the Sparkle Blue with a clean conscience."

The emperor considered this. It looked as if he would forgive her, when—

"I believe her," said Tydal.

What was the epaulette doing? The court shark was far too intelligent to blurt out of turn like that. And just as Finnivus was going to pardon her!

The emperor was equally amused. After all, Tydal had proved himself very able today and earned some current in which to swim. "What's that, Tydal? You believe her? Who cares what you believe?" But Finnivus asked this more to get a chuckle from the court. He motioned for the epaulette to continue.

"I only say that I believe her, but surely if there were any doubt, Velenka would agree to share your dangers, both large and small, to prove her loyalty—"

Velenka pounced on this lifeline. "I would! Yes, My Magnificence! It wouldn't matter how large the dangers, I'd face them!"

"Really?" Finnivus asked, growing interested. "You would share my dangers, both large and small, to prove your loyalty?"

Something about the way the emperor said those words bothered Velenka, as if they were part of some oath or code. She desperately wanted to ask questions, but it wasn't the time. "Yes! Yes, I do!" she exclaimed loudly for everyone in court to hear.

After some thought, Finnivus nodded. "It's settled then. You will share my dangers, both large and small, to prove your loyalty. If you survive, then you are surely loyal!"

Inside her mind, Velenka howled at Tydal. Just as she was going to swim free, the sneaky fish trapped her. She had to use every ounce of her will to keep smiling and not be sick. "It will be my honor, emperor! I will face any danger for you."

"Oh, you'll come snout to snout with all of them!" Finnivus said, laughing a little as he slapped his tail against the blue whale's back. "You shall swim on the front lines of my armada!"

Velenka froze her face in a smile but couldn't help gnashing her teeth once before answering. "I can't wait for the opportunity!"

"And since I nearly ate poison just now, you should eat some."

"I will bring it at once, Magnificence!" said Tydal. The deceitful court shark zipped away.

"But—but, Your Majesty!" cried Velenka. "It's . . . poison!"

She cast her big, black eyes toward the throne, but this time Finnivus was unmoved and regarded her coolly. He stretched languidly, at ease with the potentially imminent prospect of her retching death. "Come, come, Velenka. Your loyalty and innocence will keep you safe."

"I have the flank here!" Tydal said proudly, coming in from nowhere.

Of course the epaulette had found the flank of a *very* large prisoner.

CHAPTER 17

WHALEM HAD REPORTED TO GRAY THAT THE advance scouts saw the Indi armada moving relentlessly toward the Riptide homewaters. They were well into the Southern Atlantis and would arrive within a week at the most. The fevered training everyone was going through would be put to use sooner than Gray would have liked.

Takiza studied Gray. "You are quiet."

"A wise fish told me I should listen rather than speak," Gray answered.

The betta nodded. "That does sound like something a wise fish would say. But surely he meant that you should listen instead of asking stupid questions."

"The time for questions is over," Gray replied as he looked out over the cool, blue waters. The terraced greenie had been neatly trimmed and looked spectacular. The long strands of kelp floating up from the base of the cliffs were tireless, constantly waving back and forth over the lower part of the mountain as if fanning it. Gray found this hypnotic and soothing.

Takiza watched with him for a moment, then said, "I cannot be here when you face Finnivus."

"I know."

There was a long silence where Gray could sense everything happening in the Riptide homewaters. He could hear crabs scuttling in the sand, felt small fish flitting about in the greenie around the coral mounds, saw sharks moving through the waters with deliberate movements, and, of course, their mariners training in massed formation barely a thousand tail strokes away.

Takiza let out an exasperated sigh. "*Now* is the day you do not ask questions? Today? When I tell you I will not be here? You do not want to know why?"

"You must have your reasons," Gray replied. "And I don't need another worry." He felt at peace. Was that the reason for Takiza breaking him down? Definitely. And it worked. Gray was thinking more clearly than at any time since Finnivus had first come into their lives. "We can't wait for you to save us from danger every time it appears. We have to do this ourselves, or the peace we gain won't be valued as highly as it should be."

Then Takiza did something unexpected. He flashed right in front of Gray's snout and bowed deeply.

"You are no longer Nulo. I shall call you by your full, given name from this point forward. What is your real name? I do not know it as, until this point, it was not worth knowing."

Gray was taken aback, and all he could say was, "I, umm, err, I . . ."

"Well? Do not hover there with your mouth open like a sea cow!" Takiza said, acting much more like the usual Takiza. "Perhaps I was wrong to do this? What is your full, given name?"

"It's just Gray, Shiro," he told the frilly betta, who swished his gauzy fins this way and that, considering.

"I think not," Takiza finally told him. "But that is for another time. As it was, I do have much to tell you. Please do not spoil my decision of promoting you from Nulo. Demoting you in this very same conversation would be a failure on my part, and I do not enjoy failure. Understood?"

"Yes, Shiro," Gray answered. "I will listen quietly."

Takiza grunted and bobbed his head. "I went to see if something untoward had happened to the Seazarein." The betta gave him a quick glance to see if he was going to ask a question, but Gray remained still. "What she told me was . . . distressing."

Takiza didn't say anything for a time. Finally Gray said, "Okay, if you're just going to set me up like that—"

The brightly colored betta snapped his tail fin in annoyance. "I was gathering my thoughts! Sometimes you irritate me so. Never mind." Takiza took a calming breath. "You realize that various sharkkind and dwellers know me. Know of what I have done through the years?"

Gray was confused, but it seemed his teacher did want an answer here. "Yes. You're famous. I mean, everyone might not believe you're real, but plenty of fins and dwellers have heard of you."

"Correct. That is so," Takiza said. "It began when I was young and foolish. I decided that I *wanted* those who would do evil to know my name. To understand I would come for them."

"That sounds good."

"Except that it is not!" Takiza shot back. "Forgive me. I am angered by my own youthful stupidity. I now know that to work behind a cloak of secrecy, to be thought of as myth—to remain unseen, and therefore, unmeasured—would have been a far wiser current to swim."

Gray lowered his snout in a bob of respect. "Forgive me, Shiro, but I don't understand."

"There is another like myself, Gray," Takiza told him. "I, and the Seazarein, thought him dead. But he is not. It was he who sent the *fin'jaa* to Finnivus. But not because he has any allegiance to that dolt. In fact, I believe he does not regard the emperor and his mariners as a threat at all."

"He doesn't think Finnivus and his *entire* armada are a threat?"

"You saw how I dealt with them?" Takiza said dismissively.

"But that's you, Shiro—" Gray started to answer.

Takiza cut him off with a chop of his tail. "His mastery of shar-kata makes mine look clumsy by comparison!"

"Now *this* is a myth," Gray told the betta. "How could someone be better than you? That's impossible."

Takiza swam in front of Gray, thinking out loud. "It is true, I have learned and improved. I have devoted myself to the divine art. So if he lives, he may not be stronger than I am presently. Perhaps."

"There, see?" Gray said. "I knew you were overreacting."

"I hope that is so," Takiza told him.

Gray was beginning to feel better until Takiza added, "Because master Hokuu was much better at *everything* when he was my Shiro, and I, his Nulo."

CHAPTER 18

BARKLEY AND SEVERAL OF HIS BEST GHOSTFINS were shadowing a patrol of Indi Shiver advance scouts. The armada itself had been making huge progress because the currents were with them, but then, suddenly, it stopped. There seemed to be a disturbance in the royal court, but Barkley had ordered everyone to stay away from investigating it. He was thankful for any delay, but now Indi was on the move again. Any extra time was good for Gray, Whalem, Striiker, and all the others preparing for the defense of Riptide. Finnivus was just five days from the Riptide homewaters.

Barkley and the ghostfins had remained totally undetected even though they followed the Indi scouts less than a hundred tail strokes behind. Whether using greenie to mask their movements, the currents to their advantage, or swimming carefully during the night, his corps were performing beautifully.

Gray had given Barkley the important job of keeping an eye on the Indi armada since Riptide United's regular scouts were being sent to the Sparkle Blue at an alarming rate. If the ghostfins had information, one of their unit would pass a message to another scout stationed a safe distance away who would then rush back with the news. They hadn't been detected yet, even though, three times now, the royal court had lumbered its way directly over one of the unit's members.

Barkley's heart wanted to burst with pride when he remembered how the two Hammer Shiver sharks came to him after one training session and apologized for every time they had ever been disrespectful. Both the larger Sledge and smaller but quicker Peen were with him today. The hammerheads were two of his best.

The pair were so loyal that they got into a brawl with members of their own shiver when they heard a smart remark about hammerheads taking orders from a dogfish.

That was a sight to see. Even Grinder wanted a report on what happened. The Hammer Shiver leader couldn't believe that Sledge and Peen, whom he had to *order* to join Barkley's unit, were now getting into fights to defend him. After Grinder saw what his mariners had learned, he told Barkley, "Dogfish, I don't know how you've done this, but keep doing it." Though Barkley had never admitted to wanting the respect of someone like Grinder, it felt terrific.

The Indi scouts were very good compared to the first fins Barkley had ever tried to keep track of, the sharks of Goblin and Razor Shivers. Those mariners had made loads of mistakes and thank Tyro for that! Barkley got much better by stalking and watching them. He would have surely been caught by the sharp-eyed Indi mariners if he hadn't had that practice. Since then, he had gotten much better. Now, even the scouts of Indi Shiver didn't pose too serious a problem.

Although the Black Wave patrols were excellently trained, they had a series of repetitive procedures that Barkley had figured out. He had been helped immensely by Whalem. The ex–mariner prime of the Indi armada provided many valuable ideas. For instance, Indi sharks would always break backwards to see if anyone was following them *exactly* when the sun set. And sometimes their patrols would separate for ten minutes, one covering the other from above. If you knew those things, you could avoid being defeated by them.

Barkley signaled the others from his unit, staggered in the greenie below the Indi patrol, to keep their distance. The royal court and armada were passing about five hundred tail strokes to his left.

One of the other interesting things Whalem told Barkley was that the armada had a series of tail and fin signals, so they could operate while remaining silent. This also allowed them to communicate in loud places like the Tuna Run, or even volcanic flats. The signals were basic: up or down, left or right, attack or hold. Barkley took the idea and over the past few days with Mari, developed a more complete, and totally silent, signal language. It wasn't as good as speaking, of course, but the ghostfins were quick studies and could now converse to a high degree, even with its limitations.

Sledge signaled from his position among a cluster of smooth volcanic rocks. He looked like a rock himself! The trick of the sign language was an unobtrusive tail waggle that was the equivalent of saying, "Look here! I need to tell you something." Ideally you would only make this sign when you knew no one was watching, but the signal itself was usually hidden in greenie movement. It was just different enough that the sharp eyes of other unit members would pick it up, but enemy eyes would not. Sledge asked Barkley what he should do about an Indi mariner coming his way.

Barkley adjusted his position and took a look. The young mako was swimming alone, so probably not on patrol, but hunting. He didn't have the Black Wave tattoo that most Indi mariners had on their flanks, though. But to be allowed to swim the Big Blue unescorted—that was puzzling. Could this be one of the pups that attacked them at Riptide?

The mako had a symbol on his tail—an orange dot. It reminded Barkley of something. . . . Then it hit him. It was the symbol of one of the refugee shivers that had come with Riptide United.

Barkley made a snap decision that even he thought was a little crazy. Sledge signaled for him to repeat the message. Yep, it was crazy. But the rewards could outweigh the risk. Indi Shiver didn't send many patrols through the areas they passed because they moved so fast. Barkley signed once more, making sure that Mari and the two other ghostfins got the message: *Capture the pup for questioning.*

The mako was hunting in the greenie for a meal. He drifted past Sledge's hiding place. The hammerhead rose behind the mako, who was focused on a fish. With a tremendous, silent rush, Sledge struck him in the gills, paralyzing him.

Barkley joined with Mari and the rest of the unit. "Okay, we are taking this pup with us," he said quietly. The ghostfins got to work with Sledge and a large tiger, squeezing the smaller mako between them and swimming toward Riptide using the tall greenie as cover.

After an hour the mako prisoner woke and squeaked, "Where am I?"

"None of your business," Peen answered and knocked him cold once more. Although Barkley didn't approve of the hammerhead's action, he knew it was necessary. When you were out in the open ocean, miles from your friends and allies, a ghostfin had to be a hard shell.

"I don't want to question your leadership," Mari whispered when they were off to the side. "But what are you doing?"

Barkley told Mari everything he was planning, and she liked the idea so much, she sped ahead to have everything ready. He, Sledge, and Peen would remain with the prisoner.

There wasn't any talking on the way. The Indi mako was very young and scared. But anyone would be frightened to be brought to the homewaters of his or her enemies. Still, Barkley's heart went out to the pup when he blurted, "Don't eat me alive! Send me to the Sparkle Blue, but don't eat me while I'm still alive!"

Peen gave him a fin slap to the head. "Shut yer cod hole, flipper!"

Barkley was going to speak with Peen about his treatment of prisoners when Mari came rushing over. They moved off to the side where they could speak in private. "You were right!" she whispered. "Righter than you could imagine!"

"I knew it!" Barkley told her. "Where's Gray? This could be important."

"He had to leave," Mari explained as Barkley frowned. "It sounded important, too."

"Okay, we'll have to do this without him. Is Whalem around?"

Mari nodded. "Waiting where you asked."

"And our special guest?"

"Also there," answered Mari.

"Perfect, let's go," Barkley told everyone.

Their prisoner struggled between the two larger

ghostfins. "Is that cave where you're going to do it?" he said, voice cracking. He yelled at a passing dweller. "How can you live with these bloodthirsty psychos?"

It took some effort to get their prisoner to where Whalem was waiting. The special guest was kept outside for now. The mako was finally bumped and rammed enough that he stopped struggling. He still hadn't told them his name.

"Why do you hate us so much?" Barkley asked once they were inside the cavern.

For a moment it looked as if the pup wouldn't speak. But then everything came spilling out. "The good Emperor Finnivus told us about you! He said you were the ones who came and destroyed my home! You ate my mother and father—while they were still alive! Chewing up from the tail! You're a sick monster! You're all sick monsters!"

Sledge didn't take being classed as a sick monster well. He stared down the young mako and growled, "Call me that one more time. See what happens."

The Indi pup glared defiantly. "You're going to send me to the Sparkle Blue anyway. I hope you choke!"

"Settle down," Barkley said, taking control of the situation. He turned to Mari and the rest of the ghostfins. "See what Finnivus has done? He's filled these pups with lies. You grow up hearing this kind of hate and it twists you. We won't fight them. I won't send any of these pups to the Sparkle Blue."

"Well, sure as a stonefish is poisonous, they're taking a chunk outta you if they get the chance," Sledge commented.

"Yeah, what are we going to use against them in the battle waters?" asked Peen. "Harsh language?"

"No. They're going to join us." Barkley enjoyed their surprised looks as he called, "Whalem?"

The old tiger shark swam inside the cave, a commanding presence despite his age. His regal bearing and intricate Indi tattoos cowed the youngster. "Who—who are you?" the pup asked in a tiny voice.

"I'm Whalem," the tiger answered. "I used to be the first in the Line for King Romulus, commander and mariner prime of the Indi armada. I served Finnivus faithfully after his father died, even though I feared what he was becoming. I'm here to tell you these sharks are peaceful. It's Finnivus whose bloodlust knows no bounds."

The pup was speechless for a moment but then shook it off. "Liar! I don't know how you got those tattoos, but you don't deserve them!"

"That may be, son," Whalem said in a tired voice. "But it's Finnivus who destroyed your home. It was Kelp Shiver, right? Upper reaches of the North Atlantis. I recognize the orange sigil on your tail. You put up a fine fight for untrained sharkkind."

"How do you know that?" the mako asked, horror in his eyes.

Whalem's tail quivered with emotion. "Because I led the armada on that day."

The pup screamed, "You killed my mother and father!" The mako shot forward, escaping Sledge and Peen for an instant. He almost got to Whalem, who executed a savage turn and rammed the youngster into the wall. The old tiger could still fight, but Barkley could see it pained him. Sledge and Peen got control of the prisoner. They looked embarrassed that the youngling had gotten free. Barkley made a mental note to figure out a better way to keep someone still while questioning them.

Whalem said, "Finnivus ordered me to attack. And at the time there were no pup soldiers. That was something the emperor did after I was gone. I know that isn't an excuse." The tiger's tail drooped. He shook his head, despondent. "Not a day goes by that I don't think of all the horrible things I did for Finnivus. I'll never be clean! But you—you—have a choice!"

"Liar!" the pup yelled. "I don't believe any of this!"

Barkley glided in front of the pup. "I knew you wouldn't. Even though Whalem is one of the most honorable fins I know." Barkley paused and nodded to Mari. It was time for their special guest. "If you don't think we're telling the truth, maybe you'll believe someone from your *own* shiver." In swam an older whitetip with the same orange dot on her tail.

The Indi pup's eyes widened in surprise. "Aunt Larissa? Is it really you?"

"It is, Deni. It is."

Barkley didn't have to tell Peen and Sledge to release the prisoner. He had a joyful reunion with his aunt as everyone slipped out of the cave.

Barkley had met many sharks whose shivers had been smashed by Finnivus and the Indi armada. When he saw the orange spot on the pup's tail, Barkley remembered the conversation he'd had with one of those refugees. "They took our pups," she'd said. Barkley didn't know *why* Finnivus was doing that—until they faced those same pups in the battle.

"That was touching, Bark," said Peen. "But those pups are still going to come at us like crazy fish."

Barkley smiled. "Maybe. Maybe not."

ICINGHOLME
SHIVER

CHAPTER 19

GRAY SEARCHED FOR THE ORCAS OF ICINGHOLME Shiver. The Indi armada hadn't even left a holding force in the Arktik Ocean, so he didn't have to fear being discovered. Whalem said Indi had spent their time in the icy waters without meeting a single orca. The coddled emperor hated the freezing waters so much, he declared victory and left as fast as the blue whale he rode upon could carry him.

Gray couldn't find the orcas either. Orcas didn't keep homewaters like sharkkind, preferring to move from place to place in search of good hunting.

If Takiza hadn't given Gray a large dose of maredsoo, the glowing deep-ocean energy greenie, he would have never been able to make the swim. Riptide United's forces—which he'd left under the guidance of Whalem, Striiker, Grinder, Silversun, Quickeyes, and Onyx—was nearly a thousand sharkkind strong. And as rumors of Finnivus's approach spread, more sharks from small shivers from all over the ocean were coming to join them each day.

But it still wasn't enough. They weren't trained mariners and could only be counted on to do so much. And time was running out.

They needed more allies, and it was for this reason that Gray had set out. He rode the icy currents deeper and deeper into the Arktik. The crystal blue waters here were as cold as the Dark Blue, even in the sun near the chop-chop, so he ached from snout to tail. Sometimes Gray passed mountains of floating ice; other times he swam for hours with a layer of frozen water blocking him from the surface.

The main forces of the Black Wave were half a week away at the most. But there was time enough to take one more gamble to grow Riptide United's strength. Takiza told him it was a fool's errand, but Gray wouldn't be talked out of it. He had to at least try.

His idea was bold. And dangerous.

Takiza had explained to Gray what Lochlan had left out. Orcas, whom Gray only knew of from stories, really were part of the dolphin family! That hardly seemed possible. Dolphs were so chatty, and orcas were supposedly dour and close-mouthed. And then there was the size difference. Orcas were giants compared to dolphins and even the largest sharks.

Maybe they won't think I'm a big, fat freak, Gray mused. That would be a bonus.

Gray had pressed Takiza on why the orcas wouldn't help. After all, one of the most effective maneuvers in single or massed formation fighting was Orca Bears Down. Besides that, orcas were called killer whales! How could they *not* be good in a fight?

But what Gray didn't know was how the orca's history was linked to the cruel empress of the ocean, Silander, and what the orcas called "our shame." Ages ago, Silander had ruled the oceans with an iron fin until the combined forces of the free seas crushed her armada at the Battle of Silander's End. It turned out that her personal guard and elite mariners were orcas!

Their king at the time, whose name no one knew because the orcas had refused to utter it evermore, was the one who allied them with Silander. When the empress ordered her acts of cruelty, the orcas were the ones to carry them out. Some said the orca king was demented; others said he was pushed along by currents he was powerless to swim against. It didn't matter. Doing Silander's bidding was how they got their nickname, *killer whales*. The orcas stained themselves with so much innocent blood, it boggled the mind, and that became what they referred to as "our shame."

Takiza told him, "If you are set on this foolish course, then go. But under no circumstance should you ever refer to an orca as a killer whale. It is the gravest of insults, and you will most likely be eaten. And yes, they understand that killing anyone who says 'killer whale' proves the nickname, but that irony will not prevent them from sending you to the Sparkle Blue."

When Silander was defeated, the orcas dealt with their leader. After that, they decided not to side with anyone again. The rise and fall of empires and the great battles over territory would never, ever concern the orcas again.

But I have to make them understand, Gray thought. Finnivus was everything that was wrong with the ocean. He was the beating heart of cruelty and had to be stopped. As it was, Riptide United would be down two to one when the armadas faced each other. If Gray couldn't even up those numbers, at least he could surprise Finnivus with the orcas. If they would agree . . .

He had to convince them!

It had been a day of crisscrossing the territories that were Whalem's best guess as to where the orcas might be hidden. Gray wanted to talk with them, so he swam out in the open, calling out every now and again. He was, however, running out of time.

Just as he despaired of ever seeing an orca, ten massive shapes appeared out of the crystal blue.

They were awe-inspiring, giant black-and-white behemoths with huge curved teeth. Like their dolphin cousins, they had flippers and flukes instead of fins. Along with a huge black dorsal fin, each had a blowhole, using it to breathe every once in a while. Gray felt a nervous tickle swim down his spine as they surrounded him. At least half the orcas were bigger than he was, and almost all were wider and heavier.

What was I thinking? ran through his mind.

They were only a couple of tail strokes away.

The largest glided ahead of the rest.

"What do you want?" he asked in a deep, rumbling voice.

Like dolphins, orcas had their own versions of whis-tle-click-razz but could speak the Big Blue's universal language if they chose. Mostly, they chose not to.

"Umm, well, first of all my name is Gray, and it's nice to meet you."

The orca leader stared, saying nothing.

"You can introduce yourself later." Get a hold of yourself, Gray thought. "I don't know how up-to-date you are on current events, but there's a huge danger to every fin and dweller in the ocean. For the first time since Silander"—Gray saw the orcas stiffen when they heard the name—"there's an emperor. His name is Finni-vus Victor, and he's from Indi Shiver. He's insane and cruel, and his armada is laying waste to everything it swims past. I'm the leader of the free forces that want to stop him. We're called Riptide United and are made up of many shivers including AuzyAuzy, Hammer, Vortex—"

"None of our concern," the orca leader rumbled, cutting Gray off. "Leave the Arktik." He waggled a flipper, and the orcas turned to leave.

"Wait! What—what do you mean it's none of your concern? You're not concerned that innocent fins are being brutalized and killed? You're not concerned that families are getting torn apart? Even if Finnivus poses no threat to you out here, you should be concerned. He's a monster. Absolute evil."

The orca leader circled, so he was eye to eye with Gray. "Involving ourselves in your fight will only cause more death and destruction. There's nothing that can be done. Evil and cruelty have always been a part of the oceans."

"No!" Gray said. "I can't accept that. I won't."

"It doesn't matter if you accept it or not. It just is."

Gray cut his tail through the water in frustration, feeling the conversation slipping away. "You can help stop Finnivus. By doing that, you can redeem yourselves, redeem your shame."

The orca leader shot toward him in a rush. Gray had to carve a swift turn to avoid being rammed. The orca leader didn't press another attack. Instead he yelled in a booming voice, "What do you know of *our shame*, pup? A story you heard around a coral spire as your mother rubbed your belly? Who are you to come into our territory and run your mouth like you know anything?"

The other orcas encircled Gray, side to side, above and below. He could feel their anger vibrating through the icy water. There was no escape if their leader ordered an attack. "Well?" the giant orca pressed.

"What I know is that sometimes you have to swim out and be counted, no matter what." Gray stared into the orca leader's eyes. "You've fooled yourselves into thinking that not taking a side is the best and fairest thing to do. And maybe it is most of the time. But not *this* time! By ignoring *this* evil, you join with it—because you allow it to happen."

The orca leader's eyes blazed, and Gray readied himself for a fight. He let out a series of piercingly loud razzes and clicks, but deeper than the dolph variety. Gray was sure it wasn't anything he could repeat to his mom.

The orca leader gathered himself and spoke so Gray could understand. "Leave now, or die," he said in a raspy whisper that trembled with anger.

Gray moved from the circle of orcas. He wished he could say something like Lochlan could have—something that would convince them.

But you're no Lochlan, he thought.

"Thanks for listening to me. I'm sorry if I insulted you," Gray told them. "It wasn't what I came to do."

Then he left.

The swim home was long and bitterly cold.

CHAPTER 20

WHALEM WATCHED INDI ADVANCE FORCES sweep through the valley between the walls of rock that disappeared into the gloom of the Deep Blue. The main cohort would be a day or two behind them, along with the royal court.

And Finnivus.

How could I have been so blinded by my loyalty to his father? Whalem thought, remembering his friend King Romulus.

Mari was with him. *Hold*, she signaled.

It was a full thirty seconds before Whalem's far poorer eyes picked up the patrol-in-force swimming downward from the surface. Indi scouts did this to catch others by surprise. It was Whalem himself who'd observed years ago that most sharkkind didn't look for danger from above after they ate. When sharkkind hunted, they would scan for prey everywhere, including above themselves. But when their bellies were full, those same sharks would go days without an upward glance.

And now that technique is old and obsolete. Like me, he thought.

Whalem froze, allowing the tide to push him, as he'd seen Mari do. He drifted, carefully sliding past the greenie, so he didn't make too much of a disturbance even though his tail jerked involuntarily once as a phantom pain struck him. Whalem had been bruised fiercely in the Battle of Riptide. It was the beginning of his problems, for that one injury made all his others feel as if they were new again. Now, sometimes the pain of even swimming was almost too much to bear.

Mari was a few tail strokes ahead as they drifted through the seaweed. The problem was that there wasn't enough green-greenie to remain hidden and *keep* drifting. She stopped on the edge, swimming slowly against the current. While the ghostfin training was amazing, it wasn't foolproof. And not every Indi patrol was inattentive.

"Down there!" shouted a hammerhead. An Indi patrol-in-force usually numbered from eight to twelve sharkkind. This one was right in the middle. Ten well-trained mariners against an old tiger and a young thresher? That would be no fight at all.

Whalem broke cover and zipped upward, shouting, "Go! That's an order!" Technically he did still outrank the thresher. He didn't wait to see if Mari would listen but zoomed off, angling away from the patrol. The Indi mariners could still catch them both if they split themselves.

Unless they know exactly who they're chasing, Whalem thought.

"Attention, Indi mariners!" he yelled. "This is a test! Can you catch your old mariner prime?"

"It's him!" said a tiger shark in the patrol. "It's really him!"

Whalem tried his best, but the ten Indi sharks quickly made up the distance and surrounded him. For a moment, no one did anything.

The lead mariner looked at Whalem. "The emperor says you're a traitor. That you tried to kill him."

Whalem recognized the shark, a tiger from the second battle fin, but didn't remember his name. "The emperor says many things. What do you think?"

"Another of our patrols is coming," said a sharp-eyed mako.

The second group of mariners was speeding its way over. The leader turned gruff. "I think we caught ourselves a traitor—that's what I think!"

Then Whalem was rammed from behind and knocked out.

It was silent, and he saw sparkling lights everywhere. Dark blobs swam toward Whalem, but he wasn't afraid. He was happy.

And I don't ache at all! Whalem flexed his body. He felt stronger than he had in *decades*. It's like I'm a youngling again!

The shapes got closer and focused themselves into sharks, swimming between the dancing lights. They waved in greeting with tails and fins. They called to him, though Whalem couldn't quite hear what they were saying yet.

But he would soon! He just knew it!

And there was his best friend, the former king of Indi Shiver, Romulus Victor! Finnivus's father, but more importantly Whalem's best friend! Somehow whatever Whalem wanted to say to Romulus about his son wasn't important anymore. He only wanted to go swimming and hunting with his friend. And there were other sharks he knew from times long ago! That certainly was odd. Why was he meeting these sharks today? It didn't matter! They were his best friends and closest family. He would swim between the sparkles in the water and have the best of times!

It was beautiful.

But then the dancing lights dimmed.

His friends and family began to fade away.

"Romulus!" Whalem shouted. "I want to go with you!"

"Not yet, flipper," his friend told him. "But soon!"

Whalem tried to swim after Romulus but found he could barely move. His tail hurt, and his spine ached like it usually did—worse, even. Then there were other dark blobs in front of him but no dancing sparkles in the water. It didn't feel the same.

This time, there was fear.

There was one shark in particular, getting closer and closer. He felt a dull tap across his snout. Then another. The third tap stung, and he became fully conscious. Everything came rushing back. Whalem's heart sank when he saw the terrible smile of the shark in front of him.

"Are you alive?" asked Finnivus. "Please don't die."

The court joined with the emperor's high-pitched laughing. It turned Whalem's stomach.

The emperor looked over to another shark with Indi tattoos, now beaten to an inch of his life. "I will feast on your head if he dies, you fool!"

Whalem guessed Finnivus was speaking to the shark that had rammed him. Or at least the one blamed for it. "He was just doing his duty," Whalem croaked.

Whalem was chained in a *squaline* harness, an invention of landsharks given to the first Indi king thousands of years ago. These chains were useful when questioning or holding a prisoner. They hadn't put the bite blocker in his mouth, though. That usually went with the chains. Finnivus probably didn't think they needed it for an old fin like Whalem.

He was probably right.

"You're alive! I'm so happy!" cried Finnivus in mock joy. "Thank Tyro! Oh, this is going to be good."

He giggled, that high-pitched titter of his. "I've waited—
we've waited—for this day. What do you have to say for
yourself?"

Whalem had no illusions of swimming anywhere
but the Sparkle Blue. There was a rush of freedom,
sharp and invigorating, that came with this knowledge.
He shook off his aches and grinned.

"First off, when you constantly misuse the royal *we*,
you sound like an idiot."

The court gasped. Whalem thought he saw Tydal let
out an involuntary snort, but he was dizzy from his beating and most likely seeing things.

"And your laugh!" he continued. "It's the stupidest
laugh in the seven seas. Sharkkind and dwellers can
barely stop themselves from ramming their heads into
the nearest coral reef just to avoid hearing it!"

Finnivus's eyes blazed with the intensity of a thousand volcanoes. "You—you—I *hate* you!" he spit.

"That's . . . good," Whalem replied, then pitched his
voice so everyone in the court would hear. "Because if I
were a beloved member of this poisonous urchin's nest,
it would mean I'd have become evil, too!"

The court gasped even louder, then grumbled
in anger. A few of the bolder sea toadies called for
Whalem's head.

"SILENCE!" shrieked the emperor. "I'm thinking!"

Whalem got a look at the mako Velenka. She seemed
beaten down, less of a beauty than the day she had joined

Finnivus's shiver. But that's what happened when you swam in evil's wake. It marked you.

Finnivus twitched like he was being eaten from the inside. Perhaps his own evil was bubbling through his stomach. Whalem wouldn't be surprised. Nevertheless, he tired of this entire show.

"No, Finnivus," Whalem began. "You only *think* you're thinking. You see, to *think*, you'd have to possess a brain. And your head is filled with chowder. Now, I'm bored with you, so why don't you get my head onto your feeding platter? I do hope it gives you gas, though!"

There was dead silence in the court. Whalem couldn't hear anything, not even the tide. It seemed the entire ocean waited to see what Finnivus would do.

The emperor came closer and closer. Whalem prepared himself for a bite to the gills. But Finnivus didn't attack. He smiled instead, a horrible grin that showed off his brilliant, white teeth.

"You'd like that, wouldn't you?" Finnivus hissed. "It was clever, that, and almost worked. I nearly sent you to the Sparkle Blue." Finnivus looked at Tydal. "First Court Shark, bring *our* royal urchins to the court." He swung his head back to Whalem. "After all, in a nest of poisonous urchins, what's a few more?"

Whalem shot forward, trying to get at Finnivus. But the *squaline* were much stronger and didn't even need to move out of hover to hold him in place.

"Ah, here they are! Excellent!" said Finnivus. He

preened for the royal court. "I am ready to pronounce my sentence. It is . . . *mercy*."

There were shocked exclamations from everyone present. A few of the bolder ones cried out, "No!" Whalem didn't for one second believe that mercy would make an appearance today, though.

The mad emperor continued, "For all his years of service to myself and my father before me, I cannot take his life." Finnivus smiled directly at him, and Whalem felt a stab of fear. "But there must be *some* punishment." Finnivus considered, then gestured. "I will need a fin. Your left one."

"Take it," Whalem said, relieved. "Seems like an even trade to be done with you!"

Finnivus laughed. "Oh, no, Whalem. You won't be leaving just yet. The royal urchins, in addition to secreting the acid that creates our tattoos, can also give forth a liquid that will cut right though a shark's body, or in your case, a fin. But, you see, this acid from *our* royal urchins is so strong, it immediately *shuts* the wound, so you won't bleed to death. After a day, you'll be fine."

Finnivus got very close, and Whalem could see lunacy flickering in his eyes like a spastic lantern fish. "That's when I'll take your right fin. And after that, your tail. Then I will have my *squaline* drag you through the water, so you'll be forced to breathe. And my royal seasoners will put food in your mouth, so you'll be forced to eat. You'll stay alive and listen to my most musical laugh for years . . . because *we* are merciful." Finnivus went to his throne on the blue whale and nodded. "Begin!"

Whalem hadn't noticed that the urchins were already on his fin. He felt the acid drip from their bodies and howled.

But after a moment, the pain ceased, and the colorful lights returned.

How everything *sparkled*!

Then, Whalem was with his friends again, and he was happy.

CHAPTER 21

"I SHOULD HAVE DONE SOMETHING!" MARI sobbed after she told Gray the grim news about Whalem. "I should have attacked!"

"Then you would both be dead," Gray consoled. Mari swam away when Whalem yelled for her to do so, thinking he would do the same. But he didn't, of course. He saved her life with his bravery. When Mari saw the Indi scouts capture Whalem, she followed them to the royal court. She stayed and watched to the sickening and horrible end.

At one time he might have cried, but now Gray received word of Whalem's death without shedding a tear. The old tiger had helped their mariners train and gain a sense of pride. Everyone in Riptide United respected him immensely.

Now he was gone.

Along with Lochlan, and Shell, and too many others

to count, Gray thought. But all he felt was numbness. He had no more tears left.

The Black Wave was coming, and that was all that mattered.

Later that evening, by the glow of a thousand lumos, every mariner and shiver shark assembled in the Riptide homewaters. Gray could hear the tall greenie behind him brushing the cliffs below the colorful terraces, gently swishing right, then left. There were more fins than he had ever seen in one place, and all were waiting for him to speak. Word had spread like blood in the water that the Indi armada was close. No more than a day's swim now. The storm was upon them. All that was left to do was try to keep from being swept away.

The mariners were fins up and at the hover while everyone else, even the pups and dwellers, floated or perched where they could. Gray gazed at the homewaters from his position over Speakers Rock. He could see his best friends from Rogue, the trusted sharkkind of AuzyAuzy, his beloved mother and the Riptide fins, and their new allies from Hammer and Vortex Shivers. They all waited for him. For a moment Gray didn't think he could form a sentence, the weight of the moment threatening to crush him. But then the words came.

"Most of us have lost someone to Finnivus and his insane quest to form an empire." His words were soft, but the currents from Speakers Rock carried them everywhere. "If there were a way to talk or swim away from this moment, I'd gladly take it. But there isn't."

Gray paused. How did it come to pass that he was responsible for so many lives? "I know I haven't been a very good leader. No one wishes that Lochlan were here to guide us into battle more than myself. But Lochlan, and those we've lost, have gone to a better place. We don't have to worry about them anymore. We do need to save ourselves."

Someone shouted, "They're unstoppable!" There was an angry buzz from the crowd. Everyone shared this feeling, but no one wanted it spoken aloud.

Gray nodded. "It seems impossible. I know, believe me, I do. The Indi armada is big and terrifying. And we had to be saved by Lochlan and Takiza from a far smaller force because I crumbled.... But, that won't happen again. I promise to be the kind of leader you can count on. You see, I don't believe that Tyro created the oceans and everything in them to be used as a mad shark's plaything. Sheer numbers alone won't be the final word in this story. If there's just one shark with a good heart facing Finnivus and his armada, I think that shark will win. Somehow, that shark will triumph! And I see more than one good shark in front of me!"

There was a muted cheer. They wanted to believe.

Gray continued, "Together, we are *mighty*. Finnivus fights for power to crush and destroy us. But we—*we* fight for our homes, *we* fight for our loved ones, and most of all, *we* fight for what's right and good."

The eyes of the gathered fins and dwellers were riveted on him.

"We will not break, because this is our time! There are no fins or dwellers I would rather have at my flank than the ones hovering here right now. And I know something that Finnivus doesn't. I know he's already lost. He's made a terrible mistake. He's underestimated every single one of you. I know what you're made of, and it's more than he can handle. I see it in your eyes. And Finnivus will see it when it's too late. His time in the Big Blue grows shorter with every tail stroke his mariners take toward us. His black wave of cruelty and terror will crash against the mountain of our resolve. This is our home. And no one, but no one, will push us from it!"

Everything seemed to slow down, which was odd. The only time Gray had experienced this was in the middle of battle. But in a way, this *was* a battle—for the hearts and minds of everyone in Riptide United. Would they become stronger as he had because of his lesson with Takiza? Or would they shatter?

For one terrifying second Gray couldn't hear a single thing. He thought his words had utterly failed.

Then he felt a tickle.

But it wasn't a tickle.

It was a thunderous vibration—a shout so powerful it

became the opposite of loud, almost a thing of silence. The cheer swept through the homewaters. It was without a doubt the loudest shout Gray had ever heard—or in this case, *felt*—in his life. It might have been the mightiest cheer ever cheered in the Big Blue.

It was that loud.

And for the first time in a long time, Gray was filled with hope.

CHAPTER 22

BARKLEY DRAFTED BEHIND MARI AS THEY swam silently in the darkness. There were three hours before the sun rose above the chop-chop, and the Indi forces were massed just a two-hour swim from the Riptide homewaters. At sunrise the Black Wave would begin their final journey to the Riptide homewaters to launch their attack.

Finnivus meant to wipe every single one of them out.

Sledge took his turn in the lead position, or *fang point*, as Peen called it. Everyone in the ghostfins had learned to swim in close order, with their snouts under the belly of the shark ahead of them, leaving room so their side-to-side tail strokes wouldn't be fouled. Barkley had noticed years ago that when he followed someone, there was a space just behind them where it was easier to swim. The shark in front did the work of cutting through the current for the shark behind him. Barkley guessed that more than two sharkkind could move together like this, and it would smooth the current for all, requiring less work to swim through.

And he was right!

It took some practice, but once the unit learned how, close order swimming gave several benefits. Their smaller silhouette made them harder to see. And when they were in the *sea snake*, as Peen had named it—which is why the lead position was fang point—the group could swim almost as fast as a wahoo. When the shark at fang point got tired, it slid to the tail of the snake where it got the easiest swimming so it could regain its strength. Then the next shark in line would become fang point and swim as fast as it could, pulling everyone forward at *its* top speed. Sure, the sea snake couldn't carve turns that well, but if you knew where you were going, you'd get there in half the time.

The ghostfins had left immediately after Gray's tremendous speech at the Riptide homewaters. Barkley's heart swelled with pride just thinking about it. His best friend would find a way to beat Finnivus. He knew it! But they couldn't take victory for granted. For them to win, they needed every advantage they could muster. And part of that would be to get rid of one huge disadvantage.

Barkley snuck a peek up the sea snake formation past Mari to look at Deni, the mako pup mariner they had captured from the Indi armada. Whalem had known nothing about the pup soldiers and their schedules.

No one wanted to tear their way through an armada of pups to fight the Indi armada. The sharks in Riptide didn't have the stomach for that. Riptide United needed to take the younglings out of the fight.

After Deni's Aunt Larissa told him the truth about Finnivus, the young shark didn't hold anything back. He gave them every scrap of knowledge he could remember. Deni wanted to immediately swim back and save his friends. Instead, Barkley hatched another plan.

Planning something and *doing* it were two very different things. Barkley's stomach obviously knew the difference because it churned and gurgled as it warned him that his plan was suicide. But he was the leader of the ghostfins and so it wouldn't do to panic-vomit in the middle of the mission. That certainly wouldn't give an impression of calm and cool leadership. Not at all.

Sledge flicked his tail for everyone to take cover. The ghostfins silently merged with the greenie, which was thankfully plentiful in this particular area.

"There they are," Sledge whispered as he gestured with a fin at the pup mariners.

"They're almost done for the day," Deni said in a quiet voice.

The pup mariners dispersed after their drill instructor yelled the final command. They were too young to be very good fighters. Really, they shouldn't have even done such hard training at their early age. Their hides weren't thick enough for combat exercises.

But it was the several hours of indoctrination they received every day that did the most damage. During that time they sang songs and recited poems about how good their dear leader Finnivus was, and how they would take revenge on anyone who opposed him. Throw in stories about how Gray and Lochlan had eaten their parents alive, and what you got was a raging pup ready to swim the Sparkle Blue at a flick of Finnivus's royal fin.

"Okay," Deni told the ghostfins in a hushed voice. "Today was a short training day, probably going over last orders before the battle. They'll eat from what the royal hunters gathered and get some rest. That will be our best chance to talk with them."

"I still think this is crazy," Sledge said to Barkley. "If they turn on you, you'll never get out alive."

Barkley took a deep breath, his heart thudding in his chest at the truth of those words. "If that's what happens, I'll see you in the Sparkle Blue."

"I'll convince them," said Deni. "I will."

Snork nodded. "He's very convincing." The sawfish had taken Deni around the homewaters and become fast friends with the pup.

There was still the matter of the guards. Deni had had no idea that these "helper sharks," as he knew them, were really there to make sure no one spoke to them. That way the pups wouldn't be exposed to any information that might get them asking questions. "That's why we never get to swim around freely!" he sputtered when he realized the truth.

The only reason the ghostfins had caught Deni that day was because he had snuck out to do his own hunting. "Because what kind of shark has his food always brought to him?" he'd explained.

What kind of shark indeed, Barkley thought. Maybe if Finnivus had hunted the open waters by himself a few more times, he would have turned out differently.

"Okay, you all know what to do," Barkley told his team. "We are ghostfins. I want us in and out without them ever knowing we were there. You get me?" The other sharks gave a fin flick that they understood.

"Let's swim," Barkley said.

The ghostfins easily got by the patrols on the backside of the camp. Indi didn't think they had anything to fear from the direction they had just come from. That was probably true.

Most of the time, Barkley thought, as his team moved noiselessly through the water.

Training had stirred up the seabed, and there was a fine layer of silt floating in the water. This made it a little harder to see, which was fine with Barkley. In addition to the patrols, though, a pair of sharks hovered at the entrance to the rocky trench where the pups were resting. Those two would have to be disabled, not killed. Barkley didn't want to put any fresh blood in the water. That would attract unwanted attention.

Deni looked back for the go sign and Barkley nodded.

The young shark swam up to a couple of sharks that he obviously knew. They were excited to see him and yelled, "Deni, Deni!" even though he hastily *shushed* them.

Curious, the guards headed over. Barkley's spine tingled a warning. Why would they be so interested?

Then it hit him. Deni said that any shark caught breaking the rules was "dismissed" from the group.

But knowing Finnivus, they wouldn't really be dismissed. He would have those sharks *killed* just to be safe. Sure enough the guards became menacing and ordered Deni and the two other sharks to a secluded area.

Barkley signaled to his ghostfins: *Take them down.*

It was over in a fin flick. The guards were knocked senseless. Since they were a thresher and a hammerhead, Mari and Peen took their places while Barkley, Deni, and the two shaken younglings went inside to the rest of the pup mariners.

"What did the helpers want with us?" asked the young blue. "They seemed mad, like they might, you know..."

The blue shark trailed off, and Barkley finished his thought. "They were going to send you to the Sparkle Blue."

"Why'd they wanna go and do that?" squeaked a tiger shark pup.

"Because you saw Deni, and they knew he'd been outside."

"So?" asked the hammerhead. "I don't understand!"

Other pups gathered around. They were amazed to see Deni again. They had been told that Gray had eaten him alive, of course.

"Your friend wasn't eaten by my friend, or anyone else in our shiver!" Barkley said. "Finnivus has been lying to you."

The pup soldiers didn't like hearing this one bit. "Who are you to talk about our dear leader that way?" one asked.

Barkley explained further. Like Deni, the pups didn't want to believe at first. They were confused and angry.

"Listen to him," Deni told the group, quieting everyone down. "Barkley's telling the truth. My Aunt Larissa was there! She said it was Indi that attacked us!"

"You—you mean, someone is alive from your shiver?" asked a female mako.

"That's what I'm telling you!" Deni said. "And there are others, too!"

"Is that true?" another pup asked Barkley, her voice cracking.

"Name one!" demanded another.

"Okay, there's Jetty Shiver—"

"Who from Jetty?" asked a more fully grown whitetip, still at least two years younger than Barkley, though. "I know everyone. If you lie to me, you're chum."

Barkley had thought there might be questions like this, so he'd taken the precaution of memorizing a few names from each shiver. "There's a whitetip named Poole who's a mariner for us. Good fin."

The whitetip's mouth hung open in disbelief. After a moment he asked, "Are you sure his name is Poole?"

"Who's Poole?" asked one of the pups to the whitetip.

"My father," he answered. The whitetip looked around, tears forming in his eyes. "I think the dogfish is telling the truth. I think—I think—" The young shark broke down.

"Is my mother there?" asked one pup.

"Is my father alive?" asked another.

The situation was threatening to get out of hand. The pups were becoming too emotional.

Sledge scared everyone when his voice sounded from the gloom. Not one of the hundred sharks had seen him come in. "I hate to interrupt this group rub, but if you get any louder, we'll *all* be chowder."

Barkley nodded, taking control. "Sledge is right. We've got to get out of here, and we have to do it so no one notices. Do you mariners think you can do that? Can you use your training and swim out of here with us and back to the sharkkind who love you?"

There were lots of glistening eyes, but the pups all nodded.

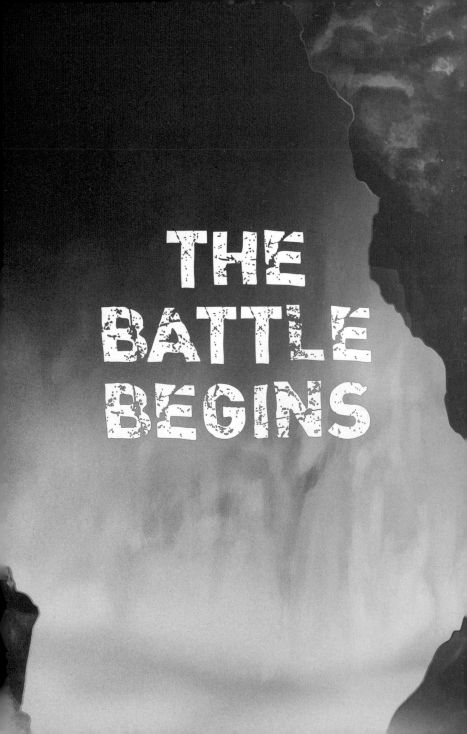

CHAPTER 23

THE GHOSTFINS HAD BROUGHT THE LAST OF THE Indi Shiver pups into the Riptide homewaters within the past hour. Gray was amazed how Barkley led his team. His friend was brilliant. Gray made the decision to move the dogfish up the Line, whether Barkley wanted it or not. He let himself smile at the image of Finnivus raging when he found out his secret weapon had been stolen out from under his snout.

And it warmed his heart to see a few happy reunions involving the stolen younglings. Unfortunately, for most there was only sadness. They found out the truth and had to experience their loss all over again. In the future, Gray thought this might be a good thing. It would make them stronger.

But to reach the future, they had to survive today.

The Black Wave's advance scouts weren't far advanced now. Skirmishes were flaring between the heavy patrols.

Grinder, Silversun, Barkley, Jaunt, Quickeyes, Onyx, and Striiker made their last-minute preparations.

The first clash in the battle waters would be important. If their forces crumbled, there would be nothing to stop Finnivus from taking the Riptide homewaters and forcing their mariners into the open ocean. There, without cover and at the mercy of random currents, they would be picked off by the larger and better-conditioned Indi mariners.

I can't let that happen! thought Gray.

"Everything is set, righty-right," said Jaunt. "And yer mum says she loves you."

Gray nodded. His mother was in charge of the pup mariners, who had to be ordered to keep from joining the fight. Gray never even considered the possibility. Just because Finnivus used the younglings as a weapon didn't make that right for Riptide United to do it. In fact, Gray would have loved to keep every one of his friends out of the fighting, behind the lines with his mother. But all of them refused.

And, Gray knew in his heart, they would be useful to have in the thick of things. He cared about Mari, Snork, Barkley, and the rest, but he also *needed* them. If they had to swim the Sparkle Blue to save the shiver, then that's the way it would go. Gray hated himself for thinking that way, but he was the leader. He couldn't hold his friends out of harm's way while asking everyone else to sacrifice those closest to them.

Gray looked down the rows of sharks from his position at the diamondhead. He saw Grinder give him a tail waggle. The hammerhead was eager for the battle. On his right, Silversun spoke to his sharkkind. The port jackson shark wasn't fast enough to swim with his mariners. Gray knew this tore him up inside, but Silversun was there now. He would be in charge of the last line of homewater defenses along with Onyx. They would send their last battle fin of reinforcements if it were needed.

"We have to win this," Gray muttered a little too loudly.

"Too right, that," said Jaunt. "We'll give them what-for, you'll see."

Striiker grunted, stretching this way and that. "Don't know about you, but I can't wait to tear into these flippers."

"You'll get your chance," Gray told him.

"I see them! They're coming!" shouted one of the forward guards.

The Indi armada swam against a light current, appearing out of the blue water in their standard pyramid formation.

But it was massive.

Gray's heart sank. He knew that they would be outnumbered more than two to one, but seeing it from barely three hundred tail strokes away was a different thing. The armada was easily more than two thousand sharkkind strong, even without their pup mariners. Gray felt terror prickling down his spine but didn't allow it to overcome him.

You have to be strong for everyone! he thought.

"Match and set formation," Gray told Olph. The dolphin above his dorsal fin click-razzed, and the command went out. Most of the non-AuzyAuzy sharks had learned which series of clicks, whistles, and razzes meant what and moved their position even before their subcommanders repeated the order. The pyramid formation was a handy starting point for a massed battle. If you knew what you were doing. If you don't muck-suck it up. Gray squashed the thought before it spread any further.

A lone tiger shark swam out from the Indi armada, which stopped, hovering against the tide like a gigantic monster. For a moment Gray didn't know what was happening, and a surge of panic arced through him because he didn't.

"Royal herald," whispered Jaunt. "For a parley message."

"You've got to be kidding," Gray said.

Jaunt flexed her fins. "Don't go. Could be a trap."

Striiker agreed. "She's right."

"I have to."

Gray swam out to meet the herald, who was terrified. Whalem had told stories about how many heralds Finnivus had doomed.

"The Emperor Finnivus Victor Triumphant wishes to tell you, umm, wishes to tell you—"

ALTBACKER

"Go on." Gray nodded.

"I'm sorry about this." The herald went on nervously, "The emperor wishes to tell you that your h-h-head is filled with chowder and you are a—a . . . fat, krill-faced, jelly-headed . . . whale that should go and hide your snout . . . in the m-m-muck with the other turtles as he, oh my, eats everyone from your home shiver. That concludes Finnivus Victor Triumphant's message to you. Do you h-h-have a reply for . . . me?"

The herald tensed, waiting for the attack he thought was sure to come. Whalem said that by law the royal herald had to remain for whatever answer came and not defend himself. Unfortunately, being herald for Finnivus meant the reply could be a bite to the gills.

Gray simply said, "Tell him I'm not going to do that."

"Is that your entire message?" asked the tiger, cautiously optimistic about swimming away alive.

"Yes," Gray told him. "You heralds have a tough job. I wish it were different for you."

The tiger was confused by the comment but quickly retreated to the royal court. Gray remained out in front of the Riptide United formation until he saw his message passed on. Then he yelled as loud as he could.

"I'm right here, Finnivus! Come off that whale and fight me! IF YOU'RE NOT TOO TURTLE!"

The current carried his words right to the royal court. Gray flicked his tail dismissively toward Finnivus and swam back to a tremendous cheer from his own mariners. Even through all the noise, Gray could hear Finnivus's shrieked "ATTACK!"

Gray smoothly slotted himself into the diamondhead position. "Way to rile him up," snickered Striiker.

"I hope so," Gray said. "I really do." Maybe Finnivus would make a dumb mistake because he was angry. They needed any advantage they could get.

The Indi armada moved, slowly at first, but then gaining speed. They came straight forward in Spearfisher Streaks by the Cliffs.

Gray thought Indi might try to end it early. During the first Battle of Riptide, the mariner prime (the one after Whalem) was too careful. He could have won the day with a crushing first blow. The delay caused by his caution allowed the reinforcements Takiza brought from the Sific to reach the fight and turn the tide.

This mariner prime was being aggressive, though. The Indi armada wasn't separating into battle fins and feinting attacks to pull them out of position. He had numbers in his favor and wasn't afraid to use them. This mariner prime was trying to destroy Riptide United with one mighty attack.

"Hake Sideslip!" Gray barked. It was a bold move in a massed formation, more of an angled attack. But being so outnumbered, Gray was forced to take chances and be daring. It turned out to be the correct call—the Riptide forces got upper position on the armada. The bottom of Gray's formation sheared through the topmost Indi mariners. But still, it was only a glancing blow, and not too much damage was done.

The two formations turned as fast as they were able. Gray saw the royal court off to the side of the battle waters, watching. Finnivus was there, enjoying the spectacle as the two armadas fought and sharks died. Gray could have sprinted his force at the court, but they would have been caught from behind. Also, the *squaline* and almost a thousand Black Wave mariners were guarding the emperor and his court. Riptide United could never batter through that in time and would be ground to chum between the two forces.

"Sunfish Greets the Morn!" Gray shouted and the order was passed on. This maneuver was neither offense nor defense but a move to get everyone into position to defend or attack. He would have to call another maneuver afterward, but right now turning speed was the most important thing.

The Indi mariners were well-trained and disciplined. They came again, barreling ahead in a Tuna Runner formation, coming straight forward to overwhelm Riptide United.

"Raise our depth one hundred! Prepare for Topside Slide!"

Gray heard a loud *fwump* noise in the water as the massed sharkkind in his formation angled upwards simultaneously for twenty furious tail strokes. The entire force climbed a hundred yards, gaining height and negating the armada's advantage of the current. Usually a Topside Slide would go into the massed formation version of a Topside Rip. Sure enough, the Indi mariners maneuvered into an adjusted Waving Greenie, ready to change that to a counterattacking move.

But Gray didn't use the Topside Rip. The advantage of Indi's larger formation was too much. They had enough fins to envelope both sides of his lines. Instead, he ordered, "Seahorse Circles, down and left!"

The Riptide United formation did a diving left turn and smashed into the right third of the armada. Gray's formation overlapped Indi's on that side, allowing Grinder's hammerheads to tear into them from behind.

Before, the current had carried away most of the blood spilled. Now there was so much, the water became a hazy shade of crimson. Gray could see at least thirty or forty Indi sharkkind spiral downward in their death throes on the way to the Sparkle Blue. There was a throaty yell of support from the Riptide mariners who weren't fighting.

Gray couldn't leave Hammer Shiver engaged for too long. The Indi mariner prime immediately ordered an Octo Reverse, trying to wrap the other end of his formation over Grinder and his forces.

"Rock Lobster Retreats!" Gray bellowed.

This move got Grinder out of danger. Hammer Shiver rejoined the Riptide United formation, which separated from the Indi armada and circled a slow turn.

Gray ordered Waving Greenie to settle everyone. His forces needed a few precious seconds to get themselves into position once more.

But Indi's mariner prime didn't allow that.

The Black Wave went through a progression of maneuvers that Riptide United would have to practice a year to do correctly: Manta Ray Rising, Sea Snake Engarde, Sea Pike Pirouette, before finally crashing into them with the devastating Cuttlefish Strikes the Crab, hitting their formation dead center.

"Break-Break-Break!" Gray commanded. Some would have tried to fight their way through, but the Indi armada was too thick. The preplanned emergency Break command split their forces into four double battle fins of more than two hundred sharkkind each. Hammer, Vortex, AuzyAuzy, and Riptide escaped up, down, and one to each side, respectively. The move caught Indi by surprise, and Gray lost only a few mariners. The damage could have been far worse.

But each shark I lose is someone I know! Gray gnashed his teeth in dismay and buried the thought. There would be time to grieve later . . . if they survived. The Indi armada stayed in formation and circled once more. There was no confusion whatsoever in their ranks.

Gray stayed with the AuzyAuzy mariners and bellowed, "Re-form diamondhead on me!"

Olph the battle dolph sent the order out. Some of their mariners were slow to get into position. They were getting tired already. The longer the battle went on, the more it favored the numbers and skill of the Indi armada.

The Black Wave rushed at them once more. They had gained precious position with their amazingly quick turn. Their top two levels of sharks were higher than Gray's! And the mariner prime didn't waste this advantage. He came at them with Orca Bears Down. Gray's formation would be ground into the seabed!

"Tripletail Turns Up!"

There was no way to stop the attack, but this maneuver regained the height they lost. And Gray's forces were now with the current! It was dead even when the Black Wave crashed into Riptide United.

Gray's sharks fought valiantly, but the Indi mariner prime had succeeded in scoring another solid hit. The battle currents flowed back and forth, the fate of the oceans balanced on an urchin spine.

Losses on both sides were heavy, but Gray's forces couldn't absorb them like Indi. If Riptide United stayed in this feeding frenzy, they would be too badly mauled to reorganize. And if their formation broke apart, it was over.

"Yellowfin Feeds on Minnows, up!"

Another risky move borne of sheer desperation.

He heard Striiker exhorting the fins under his command, "Come on, you flippers! You wanna live forever? Swim! Swim for your lives!"

Somehow, through grit, training, and sheer will—somehow—Riptide United got above the Indi formation.

Gray immediately called, "Topside Rip!" The move was very effective in a massed formation. But that wasn't why Gray called it. The real reason was, even with numbers, the Indi mariner prime would withdraw and regroup, which was exactly what happened. But after this saving exchange, Gray's forces didn't have the current in their favor.

And everyone was so tired from the fighting.

With ridiculous ease, the Indi armada reformed into a dual pyramid, the small points touching in its center. Their entire upper level was completely above Gray's highest sharkkind. This formation would snap down on Gray's mariners like the jaws of a hungry shark on a bluefin.

The Black Wave roared toward them.

"Umm, boss?" asked Jaunt.

"I know! I know!" he shouted.

They were about to be destroyed, and there was nothing Gray could do about it!

CHAPTER 24

THE INDI ARMADA CHARGED AT THE WEARY
Riptide United defenders.

Gray had a split second to answer. To flee using
Swim Away would expose their tails to attack, and they
would be torn apart. It was then he saw Riptide's reserve
battle fin roaring in from the left, taking the Black Wave
by total surprise.

Gray yelled, "Topside Slide, right!" even though their
forces were lower than Indi's. The combination of the
surprise attack by a hundred sharks and the Riptide
United forces unleashing a concentrated hit on only one
side of the enemy formation created a solid strike.

The two armadas met with a howl and a crash, both
sides ripping and tearing for their very lives. There were
so many sharkkind whirling and twisting away in their
death agonies that a constant cry of pain and anguish
vibrated the battle waters all around them. The fight

reached Gray himself at the diamondhead, and soon he was ramming and biting any Indi mariner who got close.

Though Riptide United battled ferociously and with courage, the massive Indi formation began to push Gray's forces backward. There was no way to withdraw. If the Black Wave overlapped both their far edges, it was over. Gray knew he needed to do something, but he was fighting for his very life! In the chaos of battle, he couldn't see the big picture of what was going on.

Riptide United was doomed!

Then Gray heard something.

At first he thought it was Olph, still positioned above his dorsal fin and crashing into any Indi attacker who got close. But this was different; stronger and deeper.

It was the orcas.

A pod of fifty of the black-and-white behemoths smashed into the top of the Indi armada. They struck with their namesake move, of course, Orca Bears Down. The sheer weight of the giants drove row after row of Indi mariners downward, compacting them into a disorganized mess.

"Spearfisher!" was all Gray needed to shout to take advantage of the orcas' surprising appearance. Everyone pushed forward, dealing death with their razor teeth. The waters turned blinding red.

The subcommanders in the Indi armada panicked. One cried out, "Swim Away!" Others repeated the order. Half the Black Wave retreated; the other half fought.

The Indi mariners who remained were outnumbered and enveloped by Vortex and Hammer Shivers on either side of their disintegrating formation. They broke. The Riptide United forces pursued, swimming down any Black Wave sharks they could catch, shearing off tails, and sending those fins to the Sparkle Blue.

Gray couldn't take the chance of Finnivus ordering the mariners guarding his royal court into the fray, though. "Re-form! Re-form!" he shouted. The order was click-razzed by Olph, still pressed against his dorsal like a barnacle. Whatever complaints Gray voiced before, right now he was glad the dolph was so close.

The current cleared the blood from the battle waters and Gray could see again. Finnivus and his royal court were on the move! The Indi armada joined with the rest of their mariners in an organized withdrawal. Though they were retreating, it would be foolish to pursue.

Gray knew the battle wasn't over, not by a long shot. The Black Wave would regroup and come back. And Riptide United had lost one out of every five of their sharkkind. But they wouldn't have driven Indi away at all if it weren't for the orcas.

The leader was at the head of his battle pod. Gray swam out from his position in the massed formation to speak with him.

"You came," Gray said.

"Yes," the massive orca answered. "My brothers and

sisters believe in your words. They are here, as am I, because we want a better ocean than the emperor would create. We want peace in the Big Blue and are willing to fight by your flanks for this. For the first time in ages, the orcas *will* bear down."

"My deepest thanks to you all," Gray said. "Come, we'll show your mariners to the feeding grounds and introduce you to everyone else."

"I think they'd like that. It was a bit of a swim. By the way, my name is Tik-Tun."

Gray dipped his snout in respect. "Nice to meet you, Tik-Tun."

And that was how the orcas came to join Riptide United in the first day of battle against Finnivus and his armada.

"That's what failure gets you!" Finnivus yelled at the seasoned head of his former mariner prime, neatly presented on a platter floating on a sea turtle's back.

The emperor looked at the new mariner prime. "I— *we*—hope that you do better! Or else!"

Velenka watched as Finnivus slapped the platter with his tail, and the head floated down into the royal court. Indi forces had stopped about an hour away from the Riptide battle waters.

"Yes, Your Magnificence!" replied the new mariner prime.

"Get out of my sight and prepare for a victorious bat-tle! Do you understand me? *Victorious*!"

The mariner prime was so scared he couldn't speak. He took his snout from the seabed and dipped his head at least twenty times before rushing from the court. He wasn't royalty, but a common mariner with the rank of commander. No one from the Line was dumb enough to volunteer for the job now that an easy victory wasn't in the tides. Perhaps the new mariner prime would have the skill that the previous one did not.

Velenka shivered. She had almost died in the battle! Since her attempt at poisoning Finnivus was discovered, everything was going sideways and into the rocks. If she hadn't bumped a shark at her flank into an oncom-ing hammerhead, she would have certainly swum the Sparkle Blue!

It was that sneaky little muck-sucker's fault. Tydal would pay—after Gray and his sharks were beaten. It couldn't happen any other way. The armada was just too large to lose. If only the emperor would use their numbers to their fullest! But a good third of the mari-ners remained to guard him while the others did the fighting.

"So, Velenka," Finnivus said, lolling her way. "How was your day? I see you're still alive."

Velenka smiled as graciously as she was able. "It was a pleasure fighting for your glory, Emperor Finni-vus. And yes, I am well. I only hope this proves my innocence and undying loyalty to you beyond any doubt!"

Velenka's stomach roiled with rage. *I will see you dead*, she thought.

Finnivus swished his tail absently from side to side and clicked his notched teeth together. "No, I don't think your innocence and undying loyalty have been proven beyond *any* doubt. Best to keep your place and see the battle through."

There had to be some way to improve her position! But how?

Then she had it.

"Oh, I wish you could have been there," Velenka said, flashing her own lovely white, needle teeth once more. "The experience of fighting in such a great battle was exhilarating. I must thank you. It's as if I hadn't *really* lived before this."

The emperor's interest was piqued. "Really? Father spoke of that many times. He said fighting flank to flank made the fins closest to you like brothers and sisters."

"So true," she answered, making her eyes fill with tears. Velenka could do this at will. As a pup she discovered tears could sometimes bring her what strength or guile could not. "But those beasts killed one of my battle brothers. A mariner whose name I didn't even know. Yet, without thought, he sacrificed himself to save me. Never will a day go by when I won't whisper my thanks in the waters of your empire for that." Actually, the mariner Velenka bumped had glared at her with real hate before he died.

"It *would* be interesting to experience up close," Finnivus mused. "That Gray, he insulted us. He provokes us!"

"Oh, please no!" Velenka cried out. "You're much too important to swim out with the brave and bold mariners of Indi Shiver. And Gray is such a ferocious beast! He's unstoppable. Should he see you—"

"Are you saying that I—*we*—couldn't beat a pup from the boonie-greenie in mortal combat? I'll have you know I was trained by the finest mariners in all the Big Blue. I'd have his gills between my jaws before he even realized I was there!"

"But fighting in the battle waters—while it's glorious and unlike *anything* I've experienced—is also confused and frenzied! And Gray fights from behind a line of his best mariners from a position called the diamondhead."

"I know what it's called!" Finnivus shouted. "And I have the finest personal guard in all the Big Blue! No fin, or group of fins, could ever get past my armored *squaline*! Impossible! Isn't that so, Tydal?"

The brown and yellow epaulette dipped his snout low. "That is a fact, my emperor."

What a little muck-sucker! she thought. Velenka had been waiting to catch Tydal away from the royal court and put an end to him. She was a mako after all. If she couldn't send a puny epaulette shark to the Sparkle Blue, she didn't deserve her urchin-spine-sharp teeth! But Tydal knew she was waiting to pounce and grubbed for his meals inside the court. He didn't care that everyone was making fun of him. Finnivus actually found it amusing when Tydal told him, "What better place to eat than underneath Your Magnificence?"

The Emperor swam off his blue whale and pitched his voice to the entire royal court. "It is decided then! My *squaline* and I will join the armada and command the final destruction of Gray and his traitors ourselves! Tydal, tell the new mariner prime he's being demoted. After all, who better to lead than me?"

"No one in the seven seas, Your Majesty!" Tydal swam off to give the message.

Inside her mind, Velenka rejoiced.

With any luck Finnivus would be killed and she would take over before anyone was the wiser. Her poisoning had already eliminated a few of the more powerful contenders to the throne. Indi Shiver was ripe to swim a different current, one with her leading the way.

But then Finnivus looked down at Velenka and added, "But you are right. It is dangerous. So *you* will swim right in front of my *squaline*."

"But—but—" Velenka stammered. "They're armored! Can't I be behind them with you?"

The emperor shook his snout from side to side. "Oh, I can't be losing *squaline* needlessly. It takes a long time to train a shark to swim in armor, you know!"

Finnivus laughed his insane, high-pitched titter as Velenka's heart sank to the ocean floor.

CHAPTER 25

IT HAD BEEN A HALF DAY SINCE FIRST CONTACT with the Indi armada. There were continued skirmishes between the patrols in force, but the main Black Wave force didn't attack.

Yet.

Gray was proud of what Riptide United had done, but the job was far from over. It was a miracle they had survived at all. This was a small lull in the battle. The awful thing was that Finnivus would decide when to continue. They would battle on his terms. It bothered Gray. Not because of pride, but because it was a tremendous advantage for the invaders.

There had to be a way to use his resources to win the battle. But how?

Gray watched from his position over Speakers Rock in the Riptide homewaters as the leaders of the different shivers and Lines argued their points. Everything that

could be done to prepare had been done. Their mariners waited in a loose formation, just a few hundred
tail strokes away. Gray noticed that his council meeting
was less organized, with more people talking over one
another, than when Prime Minister Shocks led them.

But he can give off an electrical jolt when he needs
to, thought Gray.

"We smashed them in the snout once," Grinder
announced. "Let's do it again!" The hammerhead gestured at Gray with a fin. "It's no secret I wasn't your biggest fan when we started, but your moves today were
nothing short of brilliant. Hammer Shiver is with you!"

"We also got lucky," said Barkley.

Striiker bristled. "Leave it to Barkley to find the rot-
ten coral in the reef."

"If Tik-Tun hadn't joined the battle, we would have
lost!" Barkley motioned to the giant orca leader, who
nodded as everyone thanked him again.

"That's true," Gray added. "And let's not forget Onyx
and Silversun sending our last battle fin in at the perfect
time to support us."

"A very good decision," Tik-Tun said in his deep,
rumbling voice.

Grinder and several others gave Onyx and the leader
of Vortex a few hearty tail slaps to the flank. Onyx was
fine with this, but the small port jackson shark winced.
"Okay, enough. My beautiful hide is delicate, you know."
This got a laugh from the group.

"We'll snoutbang them once again, Gray!" said Jaunt. "Sure we needed a few breaks, but who's to say we won't get a few in the next scrumble, too?"

Mari swished her long-lobed thresher tail thoughtfully. "True. But I'd hate to rely on getting lucky."

Onyx agreed. "If we have to *count* on luck, we're done."

Gray nodded. That was a good point. He turned the problems they faced over in his head. They were vastly outnumbered by a superior and very skillful force. Riptide United would always need the current on their side, that was for sure. Gray knew the surrounding area better than Finnivus, so that was a plus. And then there were the orcas....

Quickeyes gestured toward Tik-Tun. "We do have a brand new weapon, though. Not even Finnivus commands orcas."

Tik-Tun waggled his flukes at the group. "It is true. We can make some difference, but there are only fifty of us here. A single battle pod. And our flippers and flukes make it difficult for us to fight in formation with you who have fins and tails. At least that is how it was ages ago. If their commanders are clever, they can defend against us the next time we meet."

"No proof of cleverness from Finnivus so far," said Jaunt, which got a chuckle from the group.

Gray shook his head. "We can't let them continue to set every condition in the battle. I don't think that would be wise."

Snork nervously came closer to the meeting of the leaders. Barkley signaled him over, and pretty soon the two were whispering and flashing signs between themselves. The sawfish was a member of the ghostfins and knew their secret language.

When the pair stopped "talking," everyone looked at Barkley. "Well?" asked Gray.

Barkley sighed. "Finnivus has joined his personal guard to the armada."

There was a dismayed groan, but then Mari said, "At least they're all together."

"Right," agreed Striiker. "Just one big group of chowderheads to beat on instead of two!" Grinder gave the great white a flank bump in hearty agreement.

Barkley shook his head. "Unfortunately, Finnivus will also be in the formation . . . with every single one of those armored *squaline*."

"I don't care how tough they are," Grinder announced. "If Finnivus swims the battle waters, one of us can get to him."

"This does change things," Silversun noted. "If we take Finnivus . . ."

"By *take*, you mean send him to the Sparkle Blue, right?" asked Striiker.

"No. I don't think so," Gray answered. Everyone started talking at once but hushed when Silversun nodded for Gray to continue. "Finnivus is the emperor. If he dies, one of the Black Wave's commanders will take over and continue the fight. A fight in which we're still vastly outnumbered. But if we capture him ..."

Mari swished her long thresher tail through the water. "That's right! And from everything we know, Finnivus is very interested in staying alive!"

"The problem is that the Black Wave's losses have not only been replaced, their numbers have increased!" Quickeyes argued. "And we lost two hundred mariners. Even with the last of our replacements, we're barely a thousand strong."

Gray's mind churned. Finnivus was grouping his forces into one mega-armada. It certainly seemed like a bad thing. But by putting *himself* at risk, the war could be stopped in an instant. The seeming huge disadvantage held the path to victory! Gray cleared his mind as the others talked. An idea began to form. It was risky, but then every move against the Black Wave was perilous.

"Okay," Gray told everyone, cutting his tail through the water for their attention. "We need to fight where we have the advantages."

Silversun flicked his tail. "Advantages are nice. Do you have an idea that gets us a few?"

Gray nodded. "I have a couple. First, we need to talk to Prime Minister Shocks."

Barkley goggled. "*First*, we need to talk to Prime Minister Shocks? That's the *first* thing we need to do?"

"Definitely," Gray told everyone. His plan would

require several things to fall into place. But it was their only chance.

Silversun leaned over to Snork and asked, "Who might this Prime Minister Shocks be?"

"An eel," the sawfish answered. "The leader of the dwellers at our old reef!"

There was silence from everyone as they considered this.

Finally, Grinder grumbled, "That better be one tail-fin-kickin' eel."

CHAPTER 26

GRAY COULDN'T BELIEVE IT WHEN THE BATTLE entered its second week. His body ached of deep bruises, as well as a ragged (but thankfully shallow) scrape on his flank he received from a huge tiger mariner in close combat. There was no time to get it fixed by the doctor or surgeonfish. Gray had to be strong. Not for himself, but for everyone. If it seemed like he was beaten, their forces would wilt.

At least one in three from Riptide United was injured. So many sharkkind trailed blood that their entire formation could be tracked by scent alone for miles. And they were exhausted. When stories were told about the Battle of Silander's End, Gray assumed it was like the first Battle of Riptide, a huge clash and over the same day. In fact, he had imagined it over in an absurdly short, but dreadful and costly, few minutes. This wasn't like that at all.

The massed formations of Indi and Riptide United had only fully engaged *twice* in the last seven days; once on the first day and then again on the fourth. The mariners of Riptide United had almost been overwhelmed once again. Only a lightning quick retreat and some heroics by the orcas saved Riptide. While the Indi commander wanted to smash them, the addition of Tik-Tun and his orcas had given Gray the advantage they needed to survive. Just as they seemed to be hopelessly entangled, the orcas would roar in and create an escape path. But as Tik-Tun predicted, soon the Indi commanders learned to guard against the mighty battle pod.

The battle against the Black Wave was mostly a series of feints and rushes. Finnivus, or whoever was actually giving the orders for the Indi armada, was constantly trying to lure Riptide into battles in which they had the upper fin. Whether it was setting formations where they had the better current, or using their superior speed to trap Riptide in a position where they couldn't maneuver or retreat, there was always something.

How long had Silander's End lasted?

Maybe it went on for months....

Gray shook his head to clear it. He didn't think they could hold out for months. Or even days. Adding to their misery was the fact that the Indi armada, even though it was three times as large as Riptide's formation, was just as fast.

"They're setting up again," said Striiker.

The other subcommanders nearby looked to see what Gray would do. Things were not going according to plan. Gray had felt warm and tingly when he thought of his idea in the council meeting. But that was a week ago. Maybe it wasn't a good plan at all.

Maybe the tingly feeling was because you ate a bad fish, Gray thought glumly.

The idea hinged on getting to the Maw, but the Black Wave stubbornly refused to advance into the deeper waters. Gray knew why, too. The heavy water was harder to swim in. And it was darker there, a little scary. Consciously and subconsciously, Finnivus and the Indi armada avoided heading that way.

And Gray couldn't push them to it! That would absolutely guarantee Finnivus went in the other direction. But his own mariners were tired from the constant swimming as Indi kept checking their turns. Sooner rather than later, Riptide United wouldn't be able to withdraw, even with Tik-Tun's help. Then Finnivus would have them.

Once again, they would have to take a chance.

"Ready to attack," Gray said. "Split formation, five to one after contact and execute Swim Away." There was a slight hesitation from Olph, but then the dolph sent the message out.

There was a moment of silence in the water before Grinder shouted, "You want to do *what*?" from his end of the formation.

Velenka tensed as she watched the Riptide mariners rush forward. They had obviously been practicing and shifted their formations so smoothly now! She cursed the day she ever met Finnivus. He had placed her directly in front of the *squaline* guarding him. If the two armadas met, she could easily be ground to chum between them. But Velenka didn't plan on staying in her rank. In the chaos of battle, she would make her escape. She would swim far away, to the Arktik if necessary, and lose herself in the Big Blue. If Velenka couldn't be empress of the oceans, she would at least take her life back.

Finnivus couldn't find her then, she thought.

Could he?

The Indi subcommander shouted the commands that he got from the mariner prime, who got them from Finnivus. Velenka had the sneaking suspicion the mariner prime was changing some of the orders that didn't make sense—and saving their lives. It would mean his seasoned head on a platter if Finnivus found out, but she silently thanked him all the same. Over the last week Velenka had learned the commands well. She needed to know them to stay alive! With incentive like that, she was an eager student.

Velenka braced herself for another clash of armadas.

But at the last moment, Gray and most of his mariners swam off to the left, with just a double drove, two hundred sharks, hitting the very top of Indi's formation. Thankfully that was well away from her. They then broke off and quickly circled right and away.

"It's a fake! It's a fake!" yelled Finnivus. The emperor was swimming by himself for the first time in years, his blue whales well in the rear. The vain tiger shark wasn't lying when boasting that he'd been trained by the best combat instructors in the Big Blue. He was deadly. Before they had started this eternally long battle, Finnivus had even killed a few of his own mariners in one-on-one practice.

Velenka's subcommander got them in a formation to pursue the smaller group, but Finnivus yelled, "Don't split our forces! Go after Gray!"

The Indi armada sped up, gaining on the bulk of the Riptide mariners, who descended as they moved. The light from above began to wane as they moved deeper, toward the Dark Blue.

This is a trap, she thought.

But Finnivus had caught the scent of victory and wouldn't let it go for all the bluefin in the Tuna Run. Suddenly the Riptide mariners whirled and charged again. This time they hit the Indi formation on its right. The mariner prime ordered a flanking move, but lightning quick, the hated orcas came in and smashed them back. The huge beasts would cause even the toughest sharkkind to think twice no matter how disciplined they were. Gray's mariners retreated, swimming full speed into the blackness, downward as fast as they could.

"After them!" shouted Finnivus.

Gray set a brutal pace from his position at the diamond-head. They were close now. So close. Darkness enveloped the Riptide United mariners as they passed over the black depths of the Maw. Finnivus and his Black Wave were just a hundred tail strokes behind and coming fast.

"Turn and form up! Set pyramid fins up, hover at the ready," Gray told Olph, who click-razzed the command. The mariners snapped into position and waited. The Indi armada came out of the gloom, slowing.

"Attack!" Gray heard Finnivus shriek. "Cr-crush them!" The emperor wasn't used to the pressure of the depths and stammered because of it. Whalem had told Gray that the Indi armada didn't do any drilling at depth, but Striiker had brought their mariners here several times to train since the first Battle of Riptide. He'd gotten the idea from Lochlan, who thought that a good mariner should be able to fight anywhere. Now was when that training had to pay off.

The Indi armada picked up speed, crossing over the Maw.

"SECOND UNIT, SPINNER STRIKES!" Gray bellowed, though Olph's clicking and razzing cut through the water better than he ever could have done shouting.

Lochlan had scolded Gray for using the Spinner Strikes in a massed formation. And he was right. Theoretically, if you could attack the totally unguarded *bottom* of the enemy's formation, it would be a great move. But when did that ever happen when two armadas were fighting? To call the move was foolish because the enemy above would spot the hundreds of mariners below and grind them into the seabed.

Unless you had a giant hole to hide your mariners inside where the enemy couldn't see them!

And that was what Gray had. He had the Maw.

The double battle fin that Gray had split from his formation was composed of their fastest sharkkind. Those sharks had swum *around* everyone as Riptide United and Indi fought their way to the Maw. The two hundred sharks went down into the gloom, where the currents fell into the Dark Blue. They wouldn't be scented or seen when Indi came to strike Gray's mariners.

Gray's smaller force now attacked, roaring straight up from the dark depths of the Maw and mauling the soft underbelly of the Black Wave formation.

But that wasn't Gray's only surprise.

He had sent Barkley to speak with Briny and Hank, the devilfish. Now they, and ten thousand other small horrors, boiled forth from the Maw. With their slimy, black skin and spine-sharp teeth that seemed to overflow their mouths, they were a sight. And even though every sharkkind in the battle waters was much larger than any of these little prehistore monsters, they would scare the krill out of you if you hadn't seen them before. Gray had prepared his sharkkind for their appearance, telling everyone how frightening they looked, but not to be afraid. Briny and Hank would tell their friends to nibble on the group of sharkkind farthest from Takiza's training fields. And *this* was exactly where Gray had led Indi Shiver.

The Black Wave went into full panic mode! Indi sharks swam in all directions, fouling row after row of their formation. Some Indi mariners were so terrified of the devilfish, they tried to batter their way through their own armada, bumping, biting, and tail-whipping anything that got in their way.

"It's time!" Gray shouted. "We end this now!"

"That's the way, ya big beauty!" yelled Jaunt.

"Hammer and Vortex, open a path to their diamond-head!" Gray called. There was no named move for this, but Grinder and Silversun's mariners were very experienced. They came off the sides of the Riptide formation and hit the center of the Indi armada as planned.

The Indi mariners were frantic. They were being attacked from below and harried by scary little monsters everywhere else. It distracted them to no end, and so they weren't prepared for Riptide United's snout-to-snout assault.

Gray could actually hear Grinder's amazingly loud

"Chaaaarge!" as they slammed into the Black Wave. As soon as Riptide crashed into the formation, Silversun's commander and Grinder each called Seahorse Circles, but in opposite directions. Hammer and Vortex Shivers split the center of the Indi pyramid, creating a gap that got wider and wider.

The Black Wave was breaking. The attack at their bellies, combined with the frontal assault and the Maw creatures, was creating a perfect storm.

"Golden Rush, attack sprint!" Gray yelled. Olph the dolph clicked the command, and there was a *fwush* when the AuzyAuzy mariners accelerated as one. Gray watched the battle rage in front of him as he zoomed toward the melee. The Indi armada was panicked and under siege, but even in disarray they still outnumbered Gray's mariners. They tried valiantly to get organized. If the Black Wave managed that, it would turn the tide of the battle waters.

The fate of the entire Big Blue glided on a current as thin as an urchin spine.

It would all be decided in the next thirty seconds.

And *everything* depended on getting to Finnivus.

Gray bellowed, "For Lochlan, BULL SHARK RUSH!"

The Bull Shark Rush was used to break past a larger formation of sharks. It was an all or nothing move usually used to escape. In this case, they were breaking *into* the Indi formation to capture Finnivus.

Gray felt his blood pumping, fiery hot, from the tip

of his snout to the end of his tail. He swam as fast as he could, shooting forward as he accelerated into a blur. For a moment Gray thought he would leave everyone behind.

That wasn't the case.

Ever since Finnivus attacked their homewaters and killed their king, the Golden Rush had waited for this very second, of this minute, of this hour, of this day.

They swam like sharkkind possessed.

Time slowed. Gray's senses went into overdrive. He felt the individual vibrations when a shark down the row screamed his last scream. He heard every wail as doomed mariners from both sides spiraled into the crushing depths of the Maw. And he saw it all clearly as if it were a sunny day.

The Golden Rush zoomed into the gap created by Hammer and Vortex Shivers. Gray and AuzyAuzy tore their way past the last rows of regular mariners in front of Finnivus and slammed into the armored *squaline.*

"Defend me!" shrieked Finnivus when he saw how close Gray and his forces were. "Defend me!"

For a split second it seemed as if the sheer ferocity of the Golden Rush's charge would overwhelm the *squaline.* But these sharks were the best of the best. They stiffened their resolve and stopped Gray and the AuzyAuzy fins dead in the water. Now the battle was a straight up brawl. Sharks above and below twisted madly back and forth in mortal combat. It was like fighting inside a cave where the cave itself was *made* of brawling sharks.

The AuzyAuzy mariners fought, biting and ramming armored flanks and fins. Some *squaline* were sent to the Sparkle Blue, but many more attacks were unsuccessful because of the tough landshark armor they wore. And Finnivus's personal guard was superbly trained. Soon three and four Golden Rush sharks were dying for each *squaline* they defeated.

All would be lost if they didn't break through in the next seconds.

"PRIME MINISTER!" Gray yelled, extra loud, because Prime Minister Shocks definitely didn't understand dolphin. "NOW!"

Prime Minister Shocks was a very good representative for the dwellers. That he was an eel didn't matter for that job. But that he was an eel—an *electric* eel—did matter for *this* job. Shocks and his friends swam out from under the bellies of the sharkkind that were carrying them and struck the *squaline*, unleashing their stored electricity. Gray knew that the charge packed power, but it worked beyond his wildest dreams. Somehow the metal landshark armor the *squaline* wore multiplied the strength of the electrical bolts from Shocks and his kind, creating absolute devastation.

When they were zapped, some of the *squaline* went rigid, others twitched and jerked, and still others slammed their jaws shut so hard they broke their teeth into shards. While the landshark armor was very hard to bite through for Gray and his allies, apparently electricity had an entirely different kind of bite.

"NOOO!" yelled Finnivus. "RETREAT!"

Gray was close enough that he could see the emperor's insane eyes rolling. Finnivus wanted to swim away, but there were Tik-Tun and his orcas, hitting the Indi armada from behind. There was nowhere to go.

Gray was close enough to shout, "Yield now! You've lost!"

The tiger emperor's eyes glowed with hatred. "I never lose! I'll kill you! I'll kill everyone!"

Finnivus charged, as did Gray. Neither did a fancy or brilliant move. It wasn't the elegant dance of combat that Gray sometimes admired. No, they just crashed into each other at full speed. Gray was heavier but was stunned by the hit anyway. Finnivus received worse, yet still he came on, his lunacy propelling him with a ferocity that was almost otherworldly. "I'll never give up! I'll kill you all!" he screamed.

Gray did a quick reverse spin and landed a huge tail slap under the emperor's chin, flipping him completely around. Gray knew that Finnivus was telling the truth. He would *never* give up. Capturing him wasn't an option. Not when defeat hovered in the battle waters with each split second the clash continued. All this went through Gray's mind in an instant.

He struck at Finnivus's tail and sheered it clean off.

The fighting around them slowed.

"The emperor lost his tail!" one of the remaining *squaline* shouted. Other sharks stopped fighting, turning to watch.

Stillness and quiet spread through the battle waters. Sharks from both sides wanted to see what would happen next.

Finnivus was in shock, blood pouring from the stump where his tail used to be, thick and red. "What? Why—why can't I move properly?" he gasped and sputtered. He tried to lunge at a *squaline* to bite him. "Why aren't you fighting? You will give your life for mine! Kill someone!"

Finnivus began to drift downward. Sharks adjusted their position, opening a path for the emperor to glide downward. Gray swam at the tiger's side as he headed for the blackness below.

"It's over," Gray told him. "You've lost. Would you like me to end your suffering?"

"You'll end nothing!" Finnivus spit blood. "I—*we*—will overcome this! You'll see! I'll make *you* suffer! I will slaughter you all!"

Gray hardened his heart and stopped swimming as Finnivus sank into the darkness of the Maw. "As you wish," he told the emperor.

Finnivus shrieked, "Get over here so I can bite you in the gills! I—*we*—command it!" His raging threats continued but grew quieter as he got farther away.

Then Finnivus disappeared into the blackness of

the Maw. After a moment of silence, his insane, high-pitched tittering could be heard.

Then nothing at all.

Gray turned, and the Riptide United mariners re-formed around him. They had inflicted so many losses on the Indi armada that it was barely larger than their own force.

Gray knew he could beat them.

But it will be so bloody, he thought sadly.

A tiger shark, one of the last Indi commanders alive, swam out in front of the Black Wave's ragged formation. For a moment Gray thought he would give the order to attack. Then, the commander simply said, "We surrender."

It was over.

The war was finally over.

⋙ ⋙ ⋙

Velenka clung low by the rocky bottom and scrub greenie that grew in the depths near the Maw. The pressure and darkness were stifling, but the ferocity of the battle was far worse. She was uninjured and planned to keep it that way. The battle waters quieted somewhat, but dying sharkkind were landing every-where. Velenka was glad. It meant that no one would notice her slinking away.

Almost no one.

"Going somewhere?"

Her eyes went toward the voice in the gloom, and she saw—No! It couldn't be! The dogfish, Barkley, was there.

"Did you still want to take a fin from me?" he asked.

Velenka needed no further prodding. She accelerated to send the little nuisance to the Sparkle Blue—but the sneaky dogfish did an amazing move, slipping by her strike and landing a stinging blow with his tail to her face!

She didn't have time for this.

"Get out of my way, doggie!" she hissed.

"Take her, Mari," Barkley said and waggled his tail in some sort of signal.

From out of nowhere, a thresher rammed Velenka in the soft of her flank.

"I've always wanted to do that," Mari said as Velenka lost consciousness.

CHAPTER 27

THERE WAS A WEIRDNESS TO FROZEN LAVA ROCK. It could look as if it were still moving, sometimes jagged and sharp while other times collecting in smooth pools. Gray idly noted this as he, Barkley, and Mari swam down the rippled lava tube.

"I have to admit, I thought Jaunt was crazy to do this," Mari said.

"Yeah, but she was right," Barkley added. The three of them rounded a corner. Several lumos had agreed to stay in one-month shifts to give off enough light to see by, in return for food and a great place on a coral reef in the now very popular Riptide homewaters. "Who knew these prison cells would be this useful?" The trio glided from the lava tube into a cavern.

"Come to taunt me, Gray?" Velenka asked when they entered. The blacker than night mako stared balefully from inside one of Jaunt's reclaimed cells in what she called Riptide's royal *dungeons*.

"I can't believe you caught her," Gray said, not answering her question but instead continuing his conversation with Barkley and Mari.

Velenka was in a cell cave off the main lava tube. Thick whale ribs saw to it that she would stay put. It allowed plenty of water to circulate so she could breathe easily and even see a bit of the Big Blue through a long, thin hole. That was probably created by an air bubble escaping when the lava was hot and liquid.

"I don't know how you planned everything so completely by the Maw, but putting the ghostfins down below to bump and guide our injured mariners to safety was a tail stroke of genius," Barkley said.

Mari gave Gray a friendly flank rub. "We saved at least seventy of our mariners from sliding in. The royal doctor and surgeonfish have healed many of them. And we caught this bit of trash as a bonus."

"Don't ignore me!" Velenka shouted. "You can't keep me here! It's cruel, Gray! Are you like Finnivus?"

Now Gray did look at Velenka, and his stare made her back away.

"What are you going to do? Get away from me!" The mako shivered and shook in fear. For a moment, Gray felt sorry for her.

"Some think I should execute you, Velenka," he said.

Velenka screeched, "Not fair! I didn't do anything! I tried to help you all! I—"

Gray slammed his bulk against the whalebone bars, rattling them and startling her into silence. "Don't think anyone will believe that, Velenka! Your soul is as black as your hide."

"Will you . . . execute me?" she asked in a small voice.

"No," Gray said.

Barkley added, "Not that you don't deserve it."

Velenka stopped trembling and sniffled. Now Gray realized it had been an act by the crafty mako. "So what will you do?" she asked.

"You'll stay here for now," he answered.

"But you'll let me go sometime? One day?"

Gray hesitated, and Mari took it as a sign he was considering this. "She's evil and will only cause mischief. Or worse."

"Be quiet or else!" Velenka yelled at Mari.

Barkley smirked at Gray. "There's the Velenka I remember."

"I—I don't know what came over me," the mako stammered. "Finnivus, he—he—twisted my mind!"

"Give it a rest," Mari told the mako. "Like Gray said, we can see through you."

Gray knew Velenka was dangerous, that was for sure. And she certainly couldn't be let out for a long while. She might take over Indi Shiver if the new ruler proved to be weak. Gray heard that an epaulette shark from the royal court would be speaking for Indi when they met to discuss their future. He hoped that this Tydal, as he was called, was a peace-loving shark. Indi's mariners were still under guard, their commanders held with their own landshark chains to avoid any regrouping or organizing. And the entire royal court was under AuzyAuzy's watchful gaze.

Velenka swished her tail hypnotically. "So, what will you do, then? You won't send me to the Sparkle Blue, and you won't keep me here forever."

Barkley was about to say something, but Gray cut him off with a light slap to his flank. "You may swim free one day, Velenka. But that won't be today, tomorrow, or next week. In fact, you can count on it not happening for a long, long while." He looked at Barkley and Mari. "We're done here. Let's go."

Velenka shouted as they swam up the lava tube, and it echoed as they left. "Have your fun! I have lots of time down here, and all I'll be doing is thinking—thinking about how to get even with you! Remember this, it's what I do best!"

CHAPTER 28

GRAY WAS RELIEVED WHEN THEY SWAM INTO the brilliant sunlit waters. "Are you okay?" Mari asked.

"Yeah, I'm fine."

Barkley saw Gray was troubled and said, "It's what we have to do for now. She's too dangerous to be off on her own, unsupervised."

"I know," he answered. "Can we do something besides talk about Velenka?"

Mari gave Barkley a look. "Oh, I think we might be able to help with that."

"Follow us, please," Barkley said.

So Gray did.

And it was just what he and everyone needed.

There was a party at Slaggernacks, possibly the biggest party that the North Atlantis had ever seen. There were so many sharkkind from Riptide, AuzyAuzy, Vortex, and Hammer Shivers that a second party started at the homewaters. It was a reaction, Gray thought, to the spine-jangling fear that everyone was forced to endure since Finnivus and the Black Wave had come into their lives. Sharks and dwellers could finally stop worrying and get on with living. If it was a nice day and you wanted to do something fun, there was nothing stopping you.

It felt wonderful.

As chance had it, Gray, Mari, and Barkley got the same spot they had the last time they went to Slagger-nacks. That was the night they were attacked by the finja and Shell lost his life.

Barkley knew what Gray was thinking and bumped his flank. "It's okay to miss him, but Shell wouldn't have wanted us to be sad. Not today."

The band, which featured two bowhead whales, sang a joyous song with backup from five of Tik-Tun's orcas. Though the orca leader left for the Arktik with the others from his battle pod, the injured had remained to heal. It looked like the five were well on their way to a full recovery as they belted out song after song.

"You're right," Gray said. He moved himself upwards and caught the eye of his server. "Another round of the haddock! As hot as you can make it!"

"Aww, come on, Gray!" huffed the dogfish. "Are you punishing me?"

"You said it was tasty last time," remarked Mari, clicking her teeth together in a grin.

Barkley tail slapped Gray in mock annoyance. "That was *before* I said it felt like I was going to explode in a fireball."

Grinder and Silversun came over to their area. The hammerhead bumped him with his flank. "You ever need a few good sharks, you send word. We'll be there."

"That's good to know," Gray told him. "Thank you."

The port jackson shark gave a florid bob of his blocky head. "The same goes for me. But remember, you will never please everyone. Strive to make the best decisions and the rest will sort itself out."

Gray wanted to ask Silversun what he meant, but Grinder interrupted with a question for Silversun. "I'm going to get me some seasoned bluefin. You want some?" Both Grinder and Silversun swam off to a less crowded area.

"What was that supposed to mean?" Gray wondered out loud.

"It means youse is the big fin around here," said a gravelly voice above them. Barkley started as Trank floated into their midst from the ceiling. The stonefish could conceal himself better than anyone.

Mari frowned at Trank. "How long were you going to hover there, listening to us?"

"Not too long," Trank answered. He shook himself, and a piece of greenie fell off his weirdly formed scales. "Besides, youse shouldn't be talking about anything too important in a place where just anyone could hear."

"He's actually right about that," Barkley agreed grudgingly. He still didn't like the stonefish very much.

"And Gafin says youse can count on our support," Trank told Gray. "Getting rid of that flipper Finnivus was a good thing. A real good thing. Of course, you eat free here from now on. Kings always do."

"Kings?"

Mari and Barkley took in Gray's bewildered look and burst out laughing. Barkley gave him a good-natured fin slap. "You don't get it, do you? Gray, you're the King of the Atlantis."

"No, no," Gray sputtered.

"There's no one else anyone would rather follow," Mari told him with certainty.

Barkley did an exaggerated head bob in front of Gray. "Oh, Your Royal Muck-Suckerness, you'll have so much fun sorting out territory disputes, stopping territory feuds, and of course, deciding who will be in your royal court!"

"No," Gray said evenly. "We didn't just get rid of Finnivus to replace him with another king." Both Barkley and Mari opened their mouths to disagree, but he waved them quiet. "I am leader of Riptide Shiver, and we'll watch over the Atlantis so that sharkkind and dwellers can live in peace. But that's it. No kings."

"Do not make any plans for the future," said Takiza. "There are things you have to do, whatever you choose to call yourself."

Everyone shouted, "Takiza!"

Trank immediately made himself scarce, mumbling a quick, "Gotta check the seasonings. Enjoy your meal."

The little betta shook his fins with a flourish. "I am sorry I was unable to help with Finnivus. But I knew you would be victorious."

"What were you doing?" asked Barkley.

"That would be none of your business," Takiza answered. He looked over at Gray. "Gather two battle fins of your best mariners and those closest to you. You must meet the other leaders of the Big Blue. It will calm everyone, proving that the danger has passed. It will also prevent other sharkkind with inflated opinions of themselves from getting stupid ideas. So many sharkkind are well-versed in thinking up stupid ideas when given half the chance. We need no more blood in the water." The little betta studied Gray. "And thank goodness you seem presentable. Well, as presentable as you will ever be."

"Presentable to whom?" asked Mari.

"Why, the Seazarein, of course. She desires to meet you," Takiza said. "We leave tomorrow."

CHAPTER 29

GRAY'S MOM STAYED BEHIND, ALTHOUGH HE asked her to come along. But Sandy was now mother to all the pup mariners from Indi Shiver. She was using Barkley's unit to track down any relatives they could. This was good because the ghostfins also collected information about what was going on in the Big Blue while doing that.

When family or friends were found, the pups were reunited with them. If there were no relations left, or if they wanted to stay and become Riptide Shiver members, that was okay, too. Gray's younger brother and sister, Riprap and Ebbie, became the designated mascots to the group and now counted a hundred big brothers and big sisters.

Even without Sandy, Gray thought they were bringing far too many fins on their journey. But when it was announced that he would be touring the Big Blue, many of the major shivers insisted on sending representatives to join the procession. Gray didn't mind sharks from Riptide, AuzyAuzy, Hammer, and Vortex Shivers coming along. They were battle brothers and sisters and deserved to be there. But the others he could have done without.

As they traveled, word spread and shivers came out of hiding, many Gray hadn't heard of but which were powerful in their own right. All of them brought gifts of fish, which were welcome as they didn't have time to properly hunt. Later Gray figured out that these sharks weren't necessarily there to honor him, but to size him up.

"It's only natural. They're curious," Mari told him. "You just defeated Finnivus."

"And they want to make sure you're not a crazy finner like him," Jaunt added.

Meeting the smaller shivers in the North and South Atlantis and Sific warmed Gray's heart. They were genuinely happy to see him and, of course, relieved that the Black Wave was gone. Every territory they swam through in those areas was celebrating. The darkness was gone from the Big Blue. Their loved ones were safe and they were grateful.

Gray and his entourage avoided going into Indi Shiver's territory. Tydal, their new minister—he had refused to take the title of king—sent a representative saying Gray was welcome to come, but emotions were still running high. This was especially true because of the conditions that Gray set upon them.

First, he hadn't allowed the royal court to return to the Indi Ocean yet. They would stay in the North Atlantis as Riptide's "guests" for a year while Tydal made some agreed-upon changes. Gray also sent five hundred AuzyAuzy mariners to protect Tydal, in case one of the royals living there tried to take over by force.

The Black Wave armada was disbanded, and every sharkkind was told to return to their original homewaters. In some cases this seemed harsh, as those shivers, conquered long ago by Indi, hadn't existed for hundreds of years. But as soon as those in the armada had a chance to think it over, they understood that Gray was offering them freedom and a chance to make their own future, and they took it eagerly.

He also released the three poor blue whales that had been slaves for Finnivus's family since they were pups. It took some doing, but the Speakers Rocks were removed from their backs and dropped into a deep trench. Heaving those symbols of the emperor's cruelty from the whale's bodies with Takiza's greenie harness was the most rewarding training session Gray ever completed. The whales were frightened to be on their own at first but then heard another blue whale singing in the distance, and they eagerly swam for it.

After Tydal was firmly in control of the Indi homewaters, the AuzyAuzy mariners would leave. Gray would allow Indi Shiver to train two battle fins, no more. And those two hundred sharkkind could only be used in defense. Gray told Tydal that his forces couldn't leave their homewaters without his express permission. If Indi ventured past their boundaries for any reason, they would be utterly destroyed. Far from being angered by these conditions, the new epaulette leader seemed relieved.

This would be a hard current for Indi to swim, and it would probably take some time to sort everything out. So many of their own had died in their years of conquest. While their mariners had an idea that Finnivus was insane, the regular shiver sharks didn't like being told what to do. The Indi homewaters were filled with anger, sadness, and shame. But that was just too bad. They had caused enough trouble, and Gray wouldn't allow them the chance to do more harm. He hoped Tydal was the shark to lead them toward the light, so they would be good citizens of the Big Blue once more.

Or else.

Takiza came along on the journey, of course. He was correct to insist Gray appear everywhere. After they showed up, even though they were only swimming with a quarter of their mariners, more than a few medium-size shivers changed their plans about going to war to settle their (sometimes age-old) disputes.

Gray and his procession swam into the North Sific, toward what Takiza told them was the Seazarein's secret stronghold. Only the betta knew the way, and he led them on a winding current so as not to alarm anyone. But finally, as the sun was setting in the third week of their journey, ten massive sharkkind materialized out of the half-lit waters. They were the Seazarein's finja guardians.

"Stop the procession," Takiza ordered. Striiker ordered everyone fins up, ready for anything. But these ten sharkkind were unconcerned, even though there were nearly three hundred fins with Gray. He had a feeling that those ten could chew through everyone if they wanted.

"Come. We must go alone," Takiza told Gray.

"No way!" Barkley exclaimed. "No possible way you're going by yourselves."

Takiza gave the dogfish an appraising look. "You may join us, and Mari. But that is it."

"You give the signal and we'll come get you, no matter who's in the way," Striiker told them. Jaunt gave the great white a tail slap of approval, and Tik-Tun's orcas also nodded.

"We're invited," Gray told everyone. "Relax. Hunt. We'll be back soon."

Takiza led Gray, Barkley, and Mari toward the Seazarein stronghold. It was only a quarter mile from where they were but cunningly hidden. The thin path to the entrance was invisible, and there were groups of finja everywhere.

They swam into the mouth of the most ancient of caves. The interior was a marvel. There were giant pillars of glowing coral in a gigantic cavern. In the central area were two rows of even larger sharks, hovering on either side of the cave, creating a path to a throne. This was an actual giant throne like Gray had heard landshark kings sat upon, but made for a shark! There was a hole, so your tail wouldn't get bent and you could rest your fins, staying in one place without even hovering. It was amazing!

And on this throne waited the Seazarein.

She was much younger than Gray expected. Older than he was, but only by four or five years. She was also *massive*. In fact, she was larger than everyone in the room, even himself.

It was then that Gray's heart skipped a beat because he realized something shocking.

The Seazarein was a megalodon!

"So, it's true. I am no longer alone in this Big Blue," she said to Takiza.

"It is," the betta replied, dipping his head as a sign of respect. Takiza motioned toward Gray, Barkley, and Mari. "May I introduce the Seazarein, Emprex Kaleth, unseen ruler of the—"

The Seazarein cut Takiza off. "None of that. Call me Kaleth." She snorted at Takiza's look of haughty dismay.

"May I introduce plain old *Kaleth*, apparently," Takiza said.

"You're—you're a megalodon. Like me," was all Gray could whisper. "How?"

The Seazarein adjusted herself on the throne. "I came to these waters the same way as you did."

Gray was confused and it showed. The Seazarein glanced at Takiza. "You've told him *nothing*?" she asked, swishing her massive tail in slow, powerful arcs off the back of the throne.

"I did not want to fill his mind with unnecessary thoughts," Takiza answered. "His head is dismayingly chowder-filled as it is."

The Seazarein laughed, a musical rumble.

Gray asked, "How did I get here? How did you?"

Kaleth turned to Takiza. "Does he always ask so many questions?"

"Unfortunately."

The Seazarein looked back at Gray. "You will be my Aquasidor, my royal representative and ambassador, bearer of my word, and teeth of my will. There are many things I would have you do."

Gray was totally shocked. He glanced to Takiza, and the betta *nodded* in approval!

"But—but, your royal Seazarein-ness," Barkley stuttered, hunting for the proper title, "with respect, we need him!"

Mari added, "Yes! I'm sure this is an honor, but he's the leader of *our* shiver!"

"Not anymore," Kaleth told them. "And that's why

Tyro invented the Five in a Line. Put your first in charge."

Mari turned to Barkley, who shook his head in stunned realization as they both gasped, "Striiker?"

The guard sharks in the throne room came to attention and shouted as one, "All hail the Aquasidor! Hail! Hail!"

For a moment no one said anything. It was dead silent in the throne room. Not even the current made any noise.

Gray thought he was going to pass out.

Barkley finally whispered, "Didn't see that coming."

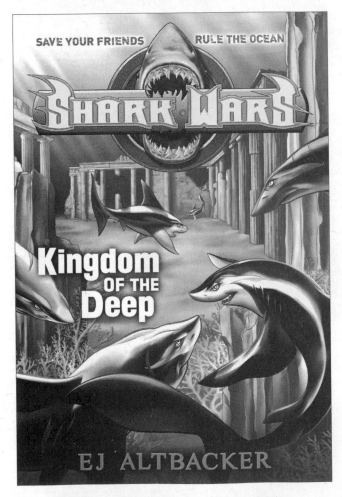

CHAPTER 1

"QUICKLY, MY SON!" GRAYNOLDUS SHOUTED at his terrified pup. "You must swim faster than you have ever swum before!"

The little megalodon wasn't old enough to speak, but understood and churned his tail as quickly as he could. Would it be enough? Graynoldus could not believe how the situation had spun out of control so quickly and completely.

It was madness!

Did the Seazarein know of the coup? Were Hokuu and the mako *fin'jaa* that agreed with Drinnok part of it? If so, the Seazarein was in terrible danger! He had to get to the other side and warn the others. Everything depended on it!

"Stop him! By the order of Drinnok, stop him now!" yelled one of the giant frilled shark guards in hot pursuit.

Graynoldus risked a look back as he made a sharp turn, guiding his young son into the narrow canyon leading upward toward the new world above. Frilled sharks were better suited for swimming in tight spaces and flowed over the jagged ridges and switchbacks while he scraped himself on the sharp rocks. The frills were part eel, and that made them very tough in a fight, especially in cramped places. They could turn quicker than any sharkkind, and though their tri-tipped teeth were smaller than his, they could tear chunks off a shark with alarming efficiency. They also had a razor-sharp spike on the end of their tails to pierce even the toughest shark hide. And they were swimming in a swarm of at least twenty.

If he and his pup were caught ...

Graynoldus kept his attention on moving upward through the twisting passage. There was no time for playing "what if" right now. He would deal with that situation if the time came. Graynoldus ground his teeth and bore down, pushing his son forward.

Fifth Shiver had been sealed off for eons. It had been so long that only in legend was it whispered that there were a sun and moon above what was called the chop-chop, a term that had lost all meaning. Their watery world was hemmed in by a limestone- and lumo-encrusted boundary. You could swim five thousand aqualeagues in any direction and no further. Such had it been from barely a thousand years after the time of Tyro, the First Fish who created all sharkkind and then set them in a Line to protect those who lived in the ocean. There were ancient stories that the Big Blue was bigger than their own waters, but there was no way to prove it.

Not until the seaquake.

The titantic quake had cracked the stone barrier and opened a path upward into the wider ocean world. A scout had swum through the falling rocks, hissing steams, and glowing lava—and made it to the other side! What he discovered was hailed as a miracle, a sign that their time was not over in the Big Blue. Graynoldus, too, was overjoyed when he swam out from the warm darkness of their pocket ocean. It had taken some time for his eyes to adjust, but he had seen the waters of the Big Blue, and the sun and moon above! Miraculous!

It was called the chop-chop because it was choppy from the waves! Who knew?

But this was a different world; much colder, the water different, but most importantly it was teeming with brand-new sharkkind and dwellers. They were younger races, but doing wonderfully.

Graynoldus's wise king, Bollagan, had decided that other than his fifth in the Line, the Seazarein, and a small group to guide the younger race of sharkkind, no one would swim into the new world until he had time to think over the consequences. Rightly, he thought that the younger races should swim their own current, with just a little help from their older, wiser cousins, as in the ancient times.

Bollagan did not want to start a war by rushing out and surprising them. If Fifth Shiver was to join the new world they should live in peace with the younger races. Yet although Bollagan was supported by Graynoldus and most others of his Line, Drinnok disagreed. He thought that they, the prehistores, as the younger race called them, had the right to reclaim the Big Blue as their own. He wanted to destroy everyone already there to the last fin.

"Let only the strongest survive! Death to everyone else!" he shouted as he sent Bollagan to the Sparkle Blue, along with the rest of the Line. Now Graynoldus was the only one left to tell the Seazarein of Drinnok's treachery! With her fin'jaa guardians they would be able to deal with him before he could invade the Big Blue.

If she was still alive.

Graynoldus used his massive tail to dislodge the loose rocks he hurtled past, but it wasn't enough. The frilled sharks, very willing allies in Drinnok's plan, were too agile. A pocket of steam blasted out, scalding his side. The path was swelling and contracting, as if it hadn't yet decided if it wanted to stay open.

"Swim, my boy! Swim!" Graynoldus urged his son as he felt a tug on his tail. One of the frilled sharks had taken a bite out of it. Their teeth were so sharp you almost didn't know you were being bitten.

Almost.

Graynoldus pushed little Gray forward and then

flipped over, blasting the attacker away with his massive tail. The rest of the frills came forward in a rush. Each time one of the swarm struck, a scoop of flesh was taken from his flank or tail. He was streaming so much blood that little Gray had stopped in shock, his mouth trembling. Graynoldus's son watched as his father was being eaten alive.

They weren't going to make it....

"Swim, Gray! Swim or you will be punished! Do what I say!"

Little Gray, frightened beyond belief, began moving upward once more.

Graynoldus turned and brought his own massive teeth to bear, snapping two frills clean in half. They went writhing and twisting into the blackness. He ground several others to paste against the rough passageway before turning to his enemies. The way was thin enough so that the frills would need to attack him face-to-face now. Though Graynoldus dwarfed any one of them, the combined strength of the swarm would tear him apart.

"You will not pass!" he yelled with all his might. "By Bollagan's mighty heart, YOU WILL NOT PASS!"

Then suddenly the mountainous walls around him cracked and heaved. An orange glow brightened the waters before deepening to an angry red.

Steam hissed, louder and louder.

Graynoldus turned and looked at his son for what he knew would be the last time. "Swim, Gray! Swim! I love you!"

Little Gray disappeared around the last corner.

Good boy, Graynoldus thought.

The frilled sharks rushed forward to finish him.

And then the world exploded.

Acknowledgments

Thanks to all the great people at Razorbill for putting up with me, but most of all Ben Schrank, who took a huge chance by choosing someone who never wrote a book before; Jessica Rothenberg, past super-editor, future super-novelist; Emily Romero, Erin Dempsey, Mia Garcia, Shanta Newlin, Bernadette Cruz, and everyone else from marketing and pubicity; also Gillian Levinson and finally Laura Arnold, my fin-tastic Shark Wars editor.

Special thanks to everyone in Los Angeles who helped me over the years but especially the awesome Jim Krieg, who I met in film school and who despite that still picks up the phone when I call; John Semper, who hired me first; Mark Hoffmeier, great writer and fantasy football superstar. Also my friends from Notre Dame, Go Irish! And finally my sister Jude, who's not the most annoying sister in the world, most of the time.

Visit **www.SharkWarsSeries.com** to learn more and to play the Shark Wars game!

EJ ALTBACKER is a screenwriter who has worked on television shows including *Green Lantern: The Animated Series*, *Ben 10*, *Mucha Lucha*, and *Spider-Man*. He lives in Hermosa Beach, California.